The Trees Beneath Us

by Darren R. Leo

Introduction by Craig Childs

*Billy,
Hike your own
hike.*

Stark House Press • Eureka California

THE TREES BENEATH US

Published by Stark House Press
1315 H Street
Eureka, CA 95501, USA
griffinskye3@sbcglobal.net
www.starkhousepress.com

The Trees Beneath Us copyright © 2015 by Darren R. Leo

Introduction: Come as You Are copyright © 2015 by Craig Childs

All rights reserved

ISBN: 1-933586-73-7
ISBN-13: 978-1-933586-73-1

Design and text layout by Mark Shepard, shepgraphics.com

PUBLISHER'S NOTE:
This is a work of fiction. Names, characters, places and incidents are either the products of the author's imagination or used fictionally, and any resemblance to actual persons, living or dead, events or locales, is entirely coincidental. Without limiting the rights under copyright reserved above, no part of this publication may be reproduced, stored, or introduced into a retrieval system or transmitted in any form or by any means (electronic, mechanical, photocopying, recording or otherwise) without the prior written permission of both the copyright owner and the above publisher of the book.

First Stark House Press Edition: July 2015
FIRST EDITION

"The early days on the trail were disjointed and without rhythm. I was reacquainting with the wilderness like running into an old girlfriend I had not seen in years. Our conversation was awkward and filled with long, unintentional pauses; neither of us the same person that had been in the relationship. In this case though, the wilderness had not changed. While my absence had been the better part of a lifetime, it was only an instant to her. She had waited. I hoped we could quickly get to the point of laughing and reminiscing and then to finding out she was currently single."

Finn is hiking the Appalachian Trail, headed south from Connecticut. He has a lot of ghosts to share the trail with—his beautiful sunny woman back home, patiently waiting his return; his kids, growing up, drifting away; a job that had "Vice President" in the title but didn't need him anymore; his breakups, his breakdowns; himself.

"How far you going?"
"As far as I can."

Introduction: Come as You Are
By Craig Childs

Escape; verb, to break free from confinement or control. I take the word with mixed emotions when it comes to wilderness, as in the natural world that lies beyond human boundaries and contrivances. What are you escaping, and what are you being forced to face?

Thoreau advised making a break from attachments before heading off for a walk. He wrote, "If you are ready to leave father and mother, and brother and sister, and wife and child and friends, and never see them again; if you have paid your debts, and made your will, and settled all your affairs, and are a free man; then you are ready for a walk."

Adore Thoreau as I must, those words have always rankled me. Why must everyday life and a good walk be entirely different things? When I first read those words, I thought, bullshit. Wilderness is not such a clean place. When you enter it, you carry everything with you.

Living a modern wilderness life, taking any snip or snatch of free time to sleep on the ground in canyons or woods, I come from a different sensibility than Thoreau. My car right now has a hatchback and back seat stuffed with a variety of packs loaded with fuel bottles and bags of dried food so that on moments notice I can launch into any number of environments for any number of days. I can pull off to the side of the road and be ten miles in by sunset. I wouldn't come cleanly with hands washed and prayers purified, all my attachments fading behind me. Instead, I come with everything I've got, every dread and hope and memory. If for a moment I can overlook deadlines and inboxes, it is only to make room for the more deep-seated parts of my life. Wilderness is not where you go to escape yourself, but where you encounter yourself exposed and unedited.

Even a luminary like Thoreau can't tell you how to come to the wilderness. You have to come as you are. Nobody living can tell you either. The picture of you in a beef jerky commercial or on a box of nature-made food bars is not the picture of you in the wilderness. You are not wearing a clean Paul Bunyan shirt or Rayon, tending to a small fire with expressionless ease on your face, nor are you on the cover of a magazine, brave explorer gritting your teeth at the tattered edge of the world. You are, instead, a human in a primal and dynamic landscape, your senses extended as far around you as they can stretch. Out here, there's nothing left to hide behind. You are fouled and scratched. Your feet stink, there's a rip in your rainfly and you've picked all the chocolate out of your trail mix.

It's a fetid mess in the backcountry, with fallen trees and boulders lying around doing practically nothing. People die out here, and not in civilly approved manners like head-on collisions, but by tooth and nail. Fingers and toes are the first to freeze, and thirst is a thing that by day three no person could sanely endure. The final loneliness, right before you are never again alone, is legendary, nothing left of you after that but food for coyotes and ravens, mulch for the soil.

Among people who travel the deeper, more primal places, you'll often hear wilderness referred to as the real world, while the other place, the one with streets, doors, and walled-in rooms that block the sky, is the fantasy. Outside is elemental, no hiding from the most basic rungs of Maslow's checklist. You'll need to drink and breathe, acts that require some effort and attention, filling a container from a spring – if you are so fortunate – or pausing, winded, with your camp loaded onto your back as you hike up the switchback of a mountain.

I once spent a month in Washington D.C., and its sidewalks nearly drove me mad. I began seeking out chipped curbs and the buckle of tree roots. I took off my shoes one day and walked barefoot. Damn the dog shit stains and dark coins of chewing gum, I needed to feel something remotely real under my feet. I found myself pausing on iron manhole covers for their impressions. A damn fool Johnny Appleseed in the city, I needed the buffer removed, and any simulacrum of a varied natural environment would save me. When I discovered actual boulders placed outside the Smithsonian, someone wearing an ID badge had to come out and tell me to get off.

You tell me where the real world is. The escape, I would argue, is into the security of civilization, with the safety of its rules and the comfort of ceaseless amenities. There, you can better obscure the demons that haunt you. For an unobstructed view of life and the world surrounding you, open the door and step outside.

Norwood, Colorado
January 2015

The Trees Beneath Us
by Darren R. Leo

Prologue

I wasn't suicidal just then. The granite extended up and disappeared into a cloud. A dark streak ran down the white face, mineral footprints of water. I studied that path. Through however many years, the water had eroded indents and depressions in the rock. They ran this way and that on their trip downward and always followed the path of least resistance. Given gravity and enough time, water would conquer most things.

To my left, the familiar white blaze was painted on a scrubby pine tree. I could tell from my stomach that it was about lunch time. Somewhere above me, the sun was lighting the tops of the clouds. I turned back to the granite and brushed my fingertips along the rock. It was rough as all stone exposed to the elements is. I found tiny fissures and slopes that belied its masquerade as a sheer face. With just the tips of my index and middle fingers on a minute ledge, I tested my weight. There was a time when they had the strength to hold me, but the technical climbing days were long gone. This face would not require ropes and belays, but it was probably something I shouldn't be doing.

I returned to the dark stain of water trail and breathed in its smell. Rocks did have smell. Granite's was clean and a little chalky. That spot had a hint of moisture although the rock was dry. Perhaps some lichen or moss up above was infusing the air. I looked at the white blaze on the pine tree and then up the granite face again. The water line extended beyond my sight; a darker path than the one with splashes of white paint. I considered and then dropped my pack. I wanted to follow that ancient trail of water, and I didn't want to squelch the return of curiosity.

The pitch was not severe. Still, while each step upward did not change the difficulty of the climb, they all altered the ramifications of a fall. I found hand holds and smeared the toes of my hiking boots into the face, and I kept my feet parallel to the earth down below so as to maximize the force my boots were applying; old knowledge resurfaced. The water trail and I moved upward. I found moss that seemed to have forced itself right out of the rock. The impenetrable stone was zero and two. From inches away, I looked at the soft, tiny leaves working to harvest sunlight. It seemed to smell green, and I wondered if colors could have odors. Insects could see more colors than humans could. Perhaps some species somewhere could smell them as well. What would blue smell like?

I was perhaps thirty feet off the ground. The height was more than adequate for a fatal fall. The sun was beginning to push through the clouds, but the rock remained cool under my fingers. A butterfly drifted by my head on the breeze. It was not a Buttercup or an Eastern Tailed Blue. With almost sky blue wings and white markings, it was another that I could not identify. I saw that a spider, small, brown and a little furry, had made his home in the moss. An inability to name spiders did not bother me, but I pressed upward so as not to interfere with his efforts to lure lunch.

A few feet higher, the water had etched a deep fissure in the rock face. It had sharp edges so it was not erosion. I peered in for snakes. That was another climbing lesson I remembered. The crack seemed to be a frost heave. I imagined a liquid army too impatient to wait out the eons of wearing down. Instead, they seeped in and expanded, a wet Trojan horse. The fissure was dry and the trail kept going so the source was still somewhere up above. The crack in the rock was about three inches wide. I stuck my hand in, made a fist, and leaned outward into the sky; making a stopper from the body part. My fist was too wide to come out of the crack, and it held me firm. If I relaxed my hand I would plunge. I looked down at my pack on the ground. Most people don't get the significance of thirty or forty vertical feet. My pack looked small. I eased up my tight ball of a fist just a little and felt it slip slightly in its stone cell. I hung out toward the earth some more. Straightening my pinky finger, the stopper shrunk and slipped a little bit more. The earth down below moved a fraction of an inch closer to my face.

The temptation was always there.

I hung there for a few moments, swinging out and away from the cliff, and enjoyed defying gravity. Soon, I felt the twinge of pain in my wrist, and I returned to sleuthing water. The dark stain of the trail continued on above me. Perhaps it was just a runoff route; a convenient path for rainwater to get to the ground. I wanted to find out so I kept climbing. A squirrel climbed with me for a while. He scampered up and then facedown the rock with his tail bouncing. In my experience, humans and the occasional cat were the only creatures that descended ass first.

At around seventy feet up, the granite face leaned back to a gentler grade, and my water trail ended. Clean granite continued upward until it reached a group of pines standing watch. I searched for signs of moisture, but there were none. Still, there was some mystery. The water had left its mineral deposit path up the cliff and stopped on solid rock. There was no crack or tiny fissure it might have been forced from. Rocks never healed, they only decayed, and that rock was intact. The water hadn't flowed from higher up. However long ago it had passed, where had it come from?

The sun was warming up the day nicely, and the clouds were breaking and drifting off to shade other places. I lay with my back on the rock and felt the warmth on my face. I dug a granola bar out of my pocket and tossed a chunk to my squirrel climbing partner. Looking down, I could see the top of the forest canopy. I had looked up at a lot of trees. It was always interesting to reverse the perspective. Here and there a coniferous tree shot up above its deciduous neighbors with vibrant green needles. From the ground, their lower branches were usually dead; robbed of sunlight by those gluttonous trees with leaves. I found a small chunk of loose rock and scratched "Finn was here. The water was not," on the granite. It would wash away with the next rain.

I liked the mystery of the water trail. It was somehow assuring to know not all questions could be answered.

Part 1

My first day on the trail, I wondered if I had wet my pants. I'd walked a couple miles, and the weight of my pack had me considering a very short meander. As I wheezed like an old asthmatic at a Led Zeppelin concert and sweat dripped into every body crevice, it was difficult to tell if I had had a bodily function activity. Concluding it would be difficult to piss up my back under the best of circumstances and recognizing that my pack was dripping, I was relieved to determine I had not pissed myself.

I labored out of the pack delved into its overstuffed contents. I discovered I had not fully tightened the lid on the water bladder, and when I compressed the pack, the water seeped up and out and soaked everything I currently owned. So, after two miles I had no water and all the shit I was carrying was wet. It turned out to be not the most inauspicious event of the day.

To say I was ill prepared that first day is to say Napoleon and Hitler made small errors invading Eastern Europe. In my Appalachian Trail version of Risk, I started out trying to hold Europe and get those bonus armies. It never worked. I may as well have had pots and pans dangling from my pack; although they would have been dry. My map, as it were, was a single fold out of all two thousand one hundred eighty seven miles of the Appalachian Trail. It might have been useful if plotting a route by plane. On the ground, not so much. Still, being pleased at the small victory of not having pissed myself, I plodded along.

Shortly, the trail dumped me onto a back road of Connecticut. I followed the white blazes on the road until I arrived at a bridge under construction. It was one lane with no shoulder or pedestrian walk.

"What the fuck," I said out loud. I tugged at my wet shorts and again considered a very short meander. Stubbornness had long been described as one of my greatest attributes or flaws, and so I stared some more at the trucks that could barely squeeze across that single lane of passage. One truck passed too near the concrete barrier. Its side view mirror was slapped back into its own window and adorned the bridge with the tinkle of broken glass. Eventually, I got up the nerve.

"Nothing to do but walk," and I scooted as quickly as I could down the middle of the bridge. Backed up traffic honked at me the whole way.

Things looked up after that. I followed the white blazes on the road as they led through rolling horse pastures lined with white fences. I stopped to pet a chestnut colt that came to investigate me. The sun was warm but not overbearing, and I knocked out some miles. Ironically, that would become one of my longest days.

The first hint of a problem was the sign that welcomed me to New York. I knew even from my near satellite perspective map that I shouldn't reach New York for a few days. What I didn't know was that road crews put white blazes on roads to signify where the shoulder lines should be painted. They looked just like the markings on the trail, and I had followed them for miles and miles.

The smart thing would have been to retrace my steps. Stubbornness worked both ways. While the trail had traveled almost due South, I had gone due West. I bought a convenience store map and planned out a southeast tack to rejoin the trail. It was a fine plan except my hypotenuse approach was twenty miles.

As the sun was pressing low against the horizon, I trudged and pondered the errors of day one. Maybe I was getting delirious. Instead of despondence, instead of flaying myself, I felt the unfamiliar sentiment of joy. It was a joy borne of being on my own, of dealing with straightforward challenges of my making instead of the overwhelming burdens of the world. I whistled as I walked, and I concluded I wouldn't be rejoining the trail that day. I had to figure out where to sleep. Call it coincidence, providence, divine irony, but I was standing in front of a Catholic church.

I had not been to confession or mass in over twenty years. Calling me a lapsed Catholic was a generous euphemism. I said an insincere Hail Mary and knocked on the rectory door. An old priest with wire rimmed glasses and wispy white hair answered.

"Sorry to bother you, Father, but I'm hoping you might help me with directions to the trail." I hoped using "father" would show my membership in the Catholic club. He looked me up and down. The plan was to ask if I could pitch my tent in the field behind the church.

"First day out?" he asked. I wondered what gave me away.

"Yes, sir."

"You're pretty lost."

He showed me our location on the map. After nearly thirty miles of walking on day one, I was still nine miles removed from the trail. Fortunately, God works in mysterious ways, or I was just lucky to find a nice old priest. He offered me a glass of iced tea, which he served with the Lipton tea bag still resting amid the ice, and he called a parishioner.

"How far are you hiking?" he asked while we waited.

"I don't really know."

"Well, how long are you out for?"

"Don't know that either, Father."

He looked me up and down. I held the string to my tea bag and spun the ice in my glass.

"Well, it's a fine summer for wandering."

I looked up at the almost perfect blue sky. A single cloud disrupted it. He chatted about long walks, and I filled my water bladder with the hose. His parishioner showed up in her truck and appraised me disdainfully as New Englanders do. Not wanting to stink up her cab or have a conversation with her, I heaved myself and my pack into the bed.

"Thank you, Father," I said.

"Try to stay on the trail."

"I will do that."

Fifteen minutes later I was at a trailhead. My driver politely inquired if I had food and water for supper which I assured her I did. I tumbled out of the truck, she quickly drove away, and I walked into the forest again. A quarter mile from the road I found a flat spot beneath a spruce tree and near a stream and declared it home for the night. I ate a packet of tuna with my fingers and looked at the white blaze on a tree a few yards away. Above me, the spruce spread wide, and I caught only glimpses of the deepening sky. I tried waiting for stars, but I was tired and crawled into my tent. Inside, I listened to the evening sounds of the forest, rustles and creaks and snaps, and I decided day one was not an abject failure.

• • •

The early days on the trail were disjointed and without rhythm. I was reacquainting with the wilderness like running into an old girlfriend I had not seen in years. Our conversation was awkward and filled with long, unintentional pauses; neither of us the same person that had been in the relationship. In this case though, the wilderness had not changed. While my absence had been the better part of a lifetime, it was only an instant to her. She had waited. I hoped we could quickly get to the point of laughing and reminiscing and then to finding out she was currently single.

I awoke with aches in every part of my body. My legs quivered and any slight movement reminded me of yesterday's walk. A lump under the small of my back, under the sleeping pad and under the tent turned out to be a pinecone. I just lay there with it pressing against my spine and surfed the web on my phone. The Red Sox had lost again. Eventually, I rose, choked down an energy bar and drank some water. What was I thinking when I came up with this idea? I thought about calling the BSW and telling her to come get me. The only reasons I didn't were pride and the fact that I didn't know where I was. I had a GPS, but it really only told me I was in the middle of butt fuck nowhere. My camp was broken down and shoved back into the pack. I was sitting on it and taking some satisfaction from the reversal of roles. I knew I was stalling. There was nothing to do but walk.

I gasped my way up a hill, digging my toes into the packed earth, and trying not to keel over backwards from the weight of my pack. Why didn't they just make the trail go around the hill? Tromping through the wilderness is much tougher than walking along a road. I stopped to check my email. There was one from the BSW telling me she loved me and to "keep on hiking." One was from my ex-wife telling me her check was late. By noon I had moved three miles from where I woke up. At five o'clock I was eight miles removed, and I called it a day. The GPS still couldn't say where I was, but it marked the distance traveled with ruthless accuracy.

I cautiously unlaced my boots and pried them off. My socks were wet with sweat and blood and whatever fluid is inside a blister. My feet were used to escalators. I washed with rubbing alcohol and winced when it entered broken skin. The feet were doctored up with bandages and moleskin. I leaned against a log, propped my feet on the pack, and the slight breeze cooled them as the alcohol evaporated. A ritual was born. Although I would soon replace the moleskin with duct tape and eventually my feet would become coarse and hard, the conclusion of each day's efforts would be the same. Before setting up camp, the feet would get a few minutes of elevated appreciation.

On the third day, I found my stick. I stopped to rest and dropped my pack. I hated it. Sitting on a deadfall oak, I looked at the carnage of its branches. It was a hard piece of wood, mostly straight, about an inch and a half in diameter, and I sawed it to size with the serrated blade of the multi-tool. It walked many many miles with me. Evenings were spent smoothing, shaping, and carving. First I whittled away all the bark to reveal the blonde wood. Using rough stones, I sanded down the nubs where branches had grown. It would become adorned with stars and rings and the names of my children.

• • •

I stared at the piles of gear on the living room floor and wondered how I'd cram it all into the backpack. It was laying there with the tags still on. It seemed bigger at the store. There were the usual camping accoutrements like a tent, sleeping bag, pad, etc. Additionally, there was a borrowed laptop, narcotic painkillers, an iPod, a GPS thing, a camera, a digital voice recorder, a solar charger, alcohol, a piece of rope woven from sea grass, and a leather bound journal. What I had, when you added up all the useful items, useless items, and shit I would eventually abandon was a ridiculously heavy pack. It was an albatross. It was Sisyphus' rock. It was other clever references to burdensome things.

"This isn't really what I had in mind," she said. I was still looking at the pile of gear, and she was looking at me. I shrugged.

"Are you sure?" she asked. I looked up at her. She had been out in the garden and had a smudge of dirt on her cheek. I wiped it off with my thumb and felt her skin. I would miss that. She smelled like basil and freshly turned earth.

"You said I needed to do something."

"Yeah, but I was thinking of therapy or medication or a self help book," she said. She looked like she might cry. She never cried. I wrapped my arms around her and held her close to me and enjoyed her smell and her warmth.

"Don't pick the squash until fall," I said.

"I know. Don't get eaten by wolves."

"There are no wolves."

"I know."

The next day she dropped me off on a back country road where a tree was marked with a white blaze. I looked at her face intently. The little crescent shaped scar on her chin was more prominent on some days.

"I love you," she said.

"But I love you so *much*."

"Shut up. Don't get lost," she said. I pointed to the white marker on the tree.

"Like that will happen." I dragged my pack out of the back seat. I looked at her; at her mostly green eyes, her eyebrows that arched up like she was always evaluating something, her tousled brown hair she told me had red highlights, but I couldn't see them, and the bright, little scar.

I turned into the woods and walked.

· · ·

I trudged into the village of Kent, Connecticut on day four. I wasn't banging out miles, but I had managed not to die or get lost again. Kent was a town with one stoplight, a grocery store, a library, a pizza shop, two competing ice cream parlors, an outfitter, and a few gift shops selling crap to tourists. Its proximity to the trail made it a frequent resupply point for hikers, and the unkempt and unclean were not uncommon.

My first stop was the outfitter. I bought topographical maps that covered the next hundred miles of the trail and a guidebook. The guidebook was updated annually with useful information like "bridge near Falls Village, CT is under construction. Detour half mile down the road." The next stop was an ice cream shop where I drank two lemonades with lots of ice before ordering two scoops of chocolate. Cold things had already become a treat.

I sat on a sidewalk bench, slurping my ice cream, looking at my map, and trying to remember how to read topo lines. It had been many years since orienteering training at Ft. Benning. I noticed another hiker making his way into town. He was an older guy, probably sixties, with a ZZ Top beard. His green pack seemed light because it looked like he carried it without effort. He was lean, and veins wrapped up his arms and legs like cables. He paused in front of me, and I nodded when we made eye contact.

"Nothing like something cold when you come off the trail," he said.

"It's good." I spooned another glob of ice cream into my mouth. Chocolate had always been my favorite although I had preferred popsicles when I was a boy. He eased his pack down with one hand and sat next to me.

"How long you been out?" he asked.

"Fourth day."

"How far you going?"

"As far as I can."

"It will be easier when you get a couple weeks in your legs. You got a trail name?"

"Um, no. My name's Finn."

"Out here they call me Treadwell." We talked for a while, and he asked me about the availability of water going north. I thought that was kind of funny. I'd spent the last two days following the Houssatonic river. I learned he was a NoBo, a northbound through hiker. He had started in Georgia months earlier and was aiming for Mount Katahdin in Maine. It was the northern end of the trail. He'd already walked over fourteen hundred miles.

I thought about that level of commitment and perseverance. I was really just wandering in the woods. He was a through hiker. The term itself implied a goal. I decided I was a meanderer. Some sparrows had settled onto the sidewalk near us, and Treadwell tossed them crumbs from his granola.

"Well, I need to get about my business," he said.

"Nice talking with you."

"Best of luck Finn. Everyone out here has opinions. Hike your own hike." He wandered up the sidewalk, and I stared after him feeling a little like Luke Skywalker meeting Yoda.

I spooned out the last of the ice cream and stuck my tongue in to lick the cup. That left a sticky brown residue on my cheeks. I didn't bother to wipe it off. I looked around at Kent and lifted my pack with both hands. I lingered by the windows of the gift shops looking at maple syrup and small knickknacks carved out of wood. Nothing to do but walk.

I made my way back up the highway carefully looking for the trail indicator. At a small and nondescript cut in the forest marked only by a two by six inch swath of white paint, I made a left and was again on the Appalachian Trail. I wondered if the people in passing cars had any idea of the thoroughfare they were driving by. Thousands of people hiked big chunks of the trail every year. A few hundred would walk its entirety. Some large number of people with packs crossed that highway and disappeared through the cut. Each had a purpose. Some had dreams. All had reasons. At best, they'd get a cursory glance from someone in a car. I paused for a moment with one foot in the shadow of a maple tree and the other in the sunlit, clear cut side of the road. I flipped the bird at the next car that passed then I turned and entered the forest. The car was a Lexus.

That night I pitched my tent in a young forest on the crest of a hill. Amid the skinny trunks, I looked up at the slices of sky. I'd watched the sky from many angles; none of them far enough apart to change the perspective. When stars are trillions of light years apart, viewing them from one side of the earth or the other won't really matter. I'd seen the stars from a red desert in Utah where they were thick like bees on a hive, and I could see satellites making their rounds. I had seen the stars from atop a skyscraper in Manhattan on a clear night and could still count them all on my fingers.

Hike your own hike. I thought about refinancing mortgages, organizing funerals and paying attorney fees. Hike your own hike. It had been a long time since I'd done so. I waited and, a little past hiker's midnight which was eight p.m., Orion's belt glowed through a crack in the canopy above, and I thought about camping with Keegan when he was about five years old. I didn't take Trazodone that night, but I still slept until almost three.

• • •

Keegan entered the world on a muggy morning in August. We took him home and had no clue what to do. We changed diapers, and he peed on me. We attached him to a boob to eat. Well, she really did that part. We spent a lot of time grinning at him and speaking in tones we couldn't understand; but we expected him to.

At around six months old, he decided sleeping wasn't really for him. I put him, in his bassinet, on the dryer. I put him in his car seat and drove him around the neighborhood. I held him close and danced around the living room. Nothing except exhaustion made him fall asleep. We made frantic calls to the pediatrician and were reassured that everything was fine.

I was in my last semester of school then. I needed six credits, and I took a macroeconomics class and one on "great books". I signed up thinking it would be *Moby Dick* and *A Tale of Two Cities* or other books I'd read already. It wasn't. I kept Keegan with me during the day while his mom was at work. I took odd jobs my father didn't have time for; building a deck, drywalling a basement, tearing down a covered porch. Keegan accompanied me strapped to my back. When winter came, we shoveled driveways. When winter really came, I devised a tool of u shaped metal attached to a strip of plastic. Shoved on a sagging roof, it broke up the snow and made it slide off. Hours of shoveling were accomplished in minutes. I was quite proud of that. I went to class in the evening and came home to hold Keegan and read *Heat and Dust* or *The Beantrees*.

On a frigid night in February I discovered the cure for Keegan' insomnia. It was about two a.m., and we had been working on the impact of price elasticity on demand for gasoline. That is to say, I held him with one arm and he played with the buttons on my shirt while I scribbled with my other arm. The full moon was gleaming through the window. I bundled him up, and we went out into the sharp night. The snow squeaked beneath my boots. It was a clear night, and I gazed at the stars with my son cradled in my arms. When I looked down I saw that he too was gazing at the stars. His little face was wide with wonder, and I shared his awe at seeing the night sky for the first time.

I pointed out Polaris, the North star, and explained how you could use it to navigate. I showed him Ursa Major and Ursa Minor; the big and little bears. I told him how the light from some stars took millions of years to reach us, and those stars might not even be there anymore. We looked at Pegasus and the Winter Triangle. The three bright stars of Orion's belt glistened directly over our heads, and Keegan seemed to stare at them before promptly falling asleep.

Every night we would go out to peer at the stars of Keegan' sky, and he would slip into sleep with Orion peering down.

• • •

Over time, I had dinner with Mocha Crow, Tadpole, Clarity, and others. I shared water with Chopsticks and GI. I met MacGyver's Mother. I traded trail information with Pollylog, Mowgli and Babaganoosh.

Thor gave me directions. I never learned if GI was for government issued or gastrointestinal; maybe both. Hikers rarely went by their real names. They adopted, or were given, a trail name. It was important to adopt one. If not, one might end up as Dumbass or Sir Shits a Lot.

I found the trail name concept fascinating. It was like extended Halloween only with trees and ticks instead of Smarties and Snickers. While we were out there, we got to be someone other than ourselves; perhaps a better version of ourselves. It was a fresh start. A lifetime of baggage, successes and failures was left behind at least for a time. Or so I hoped. Yet I was resistant to the trail name. Even after taking one on, I still introduced myself as Finn. Perhaps it was penance. Maybe it was a feeling of guilt that I shouldn't be allowed to just abandon all the failures; I should drag them along, an albatross far heavier than the backpack. Eventually, I began using my trail name just to avoid awkward conversations.

"I'm Ivan the Hiking Viking," some hiker might say.

"I'm Finn."

Long pause.

"Oh, my name is Bob," he would reply.

So, I became Polar. My name fueled much speculation among the hikers I met. Did it reference bears or icecaps? I occasionally suggested bipolar as it described the love hate relationship with the trail. In truth, it was an acronym: Path of Least Resistance. It came about from a conversation with the BSW when I told her I was going to go hike the trail.

"Are you sure it's a good idea?" she asked. I was quiet. It was a dreary, wet day, and the sound of rain and wind outside echoed in the living room. She was sitting on the couch with her legs curled under her and covered with her favorite blanket and two cats.

"Are there bears?" she asked.

"Only small ones."

"What if you have a flare up or get hurt?"

"I'll take the path of least resistance. Like water."

"The path of least resistance would be to stay home."

· · ·

A little north of the Hudson river in New York, I went off the trail again. My destination was Graymoor monastery. According to my guidebook, it was home to the Franciscan Friars of the Atonement, and they welcomed hikers. I was nine days into meandering, and I was tired. It was time for my first zero day. And me going to a monastery of atonement was some funny shit.

The monastery was an old flagstone building with spires and sharply slanted roof lines going every which way. At some point they added on a square brick wing to house drug addicts and ruin the architecture. Down the hill they had a combination baseball diamond, soccer field, and garden, and that was where the hikers stayed. There was a pavilion with electric lights and picnic tables, a pump with cold clean water, a shower enclosed by wood slats, and a porta potty.

There were a couple hikers in the pavilion when I showed up. The one wearing a kilt had arms tattooed with Celtic symbols, and although his hairline had receded to the middle of his head, the remaining hair was twisted into long dreadlocks. The other was wearing red satin pants, an unbuttoned green satin shirt and had strange welts on his skin. I pitched my tent a good distance away.

I consulted the oracle, the guidebook, and saw there was a convenience store two miles away so I gave my feet their moment of rest, slipped on the flip flops and walked down. It was not lost on me that a couple weeks prior I would have considered a four mile round trip to the mini mart a significant task. I bought chocolate chip cookies, a six pack of Heineken in little keg shaped cans, and a turkey sandwich with droopy lettuce and a mushy tomato. I took extra packets of mustard and hot sauce. They were useful for doctoring trail meals. Without the pack or boots, the walk was easy, and I found myself moving at a good clip and still noticing things like a shiny rock I paused to investigate.

Back at the ball field I sprawled on the ground and enjoyed the feeling of grass. I was in the shade of a hulking elm tree, and sparrows chattered above me. I sipped a lukewarm beer and concluded I was well equipped for a zero day. A zero day is zero mileage; a day of rest. They were carefully planned and looked forward to by the through hikers. Those people had places to go. I could have taken many zero days, but I was driven by a simple need to keep moving, to keep putting distance behind me. I threw bread crumbs at the base of the tree to lure down a chipmunk.

It was a busy day in the pavilion. The first wave of NoBo's was reaching New York, and several hikers came and went. A couple hiked in. He was tall, with a thick beard, and spoke with a German accent. She was a small Asian woman with hairy legs. They dropped their packs, unrolled their sleeping pads, slept for a couple hours and left. The creepy carnival guys passed a joint back and forth. A friar came down the hill and visited with those in the pavilion. I watched from my place by the tree.

I awoke again in the middle of the night. That time it was not because of the monastery's bells that chimed every damn hour. It was the throbbing pain in my hand and foot. I had been waiting for an arthritis flare up.

They always came.

I crawled out of the tent which seemed hot and too enclosed, put my feet up on the pack and my hand on my heart like I was saying the pledge of allegiance. Remaining very still, I could make out the three types of RA pain. The inflammation was like sticking a knuckle on a hot stove and holding it there until the skin starts to cook. The dull ache pain emanated as if right from the marrow. The searing, shooting pain happened when I attempted anything my body didn't want to do like zip my pants or generally move in any way. It was like being stabbed with a hot fireplace poker. I assumed that because I hadn't been stabbed by a hot fireplace poker. When all three sorts of pain were occurring at once, it's called a flare up, and the rheumatologist would give me restricted narcotics and a pitying look.

The narcotics did very little to alleviate the pain. What they did accomplish admirably was made me not care much about it. They also removed most social inhibitions, all good judgment and inhibited one's ability to operate heavy machinery. I imagined that was frustrating for backhoe operators.

So, I rolled over, rummaged through the pack and considered if it was going to be a Vicodin or Percocet night. I decided on the Percocet, then on two of them and returned to my prone, patriotic position for the long and incoherent vigil. I could feel my pulse in my hand, and each heartbeat sent a surge of pain. I dozed in fits; waking every time I moved or when the church bells chimed. Each time I struggled to recall where I was and then wondered why I was there. I gave up trying to sleep and lay absolutely still looking up at the dark outline of the tree and trying to remember the words to the pledge of allegiance.

"Hi," she answered when I made my morning call to the BSW to assure her I was still alive.

"Hi honey." I tried to make my voice sound normal. The narcotics made me talk slowly and slur.

"Are you on Percocet?"

"Small flare up."

"Are you safe?"

"I'm at a monastery."

She googled Greymoor and told me about the work they did with the indigent. The day off allowed me to fill the solar charger and subsequently get a good charge on the phone so we talked longer than normal. She told me about her new client and how annoying my dog was being. It already seemed so long since I'd seen her. We said our love you's.

"Be careful," she said.

"You know me."

"Exactly."

I spent my zero day mostly in my tent. I studied my maps and read ahead in the guidebook. I didn't remember much of what I read so it allowed me to do it over and over without getting bored. I occasionally hobbled to the pump to fill my water bottle. I had previously considered what I'd do if a flare up came while I was high on a ridgeline and miles from water. I'd crawl across that bridge when I came to it.

One of the creepy carnival guys approached me; the balding one with dreadlocks. I checked to see that my walking stick was close.

"You okay, man?" he asked.

"What?"

"I saw you were limping. You okay?"

"Just a little sore." I never shared details about my disease.

"Want me to fill your water bottle?"

"Uh, thanks. That'd be great."

"Beautiful day," he said.

"Yeah, it is." I looked down at blades of grass.

"If you need anything, just shout."

"Thank you."

Over in the pavilion, he and the other guy pulled out flutes and played beautiful and haunting melodies. I had never been good at judging people.

· · ·

I had been to a corporate retreat; one of those things meant to inspire and reward but mostly involved a lot of drinking at the open bar and bullshit team building exercises. I believed one of the primary functions of such events was the creation of new buzzwords. How else to explain "deliverable"? I pictured it coming from a group of middle aged executives sitting at the bar of the Sheraton having just concluded the ropes course where they had to solve the dilemma of getting the three hundred pound guy from accounts payable over a ravine.

At that particular retreat we played bongo drums. I had no idea what I was supposed to learn about my job, but banging on a drum was pretty fun. The day after beating on a drum my hands were swollen. I thought little of it and figured it was because I was a neophyte drum banger. A couple days later I returned home with a massive hangover and still swollen hands.

When they didn't stop hurting, I finally went to the doctor. I had once dislocated two fingers rock climbing. There was a certain honor in telling the doctor that the injury occurred on the side of a cliff. Banging on a drum, not so much. So, when my doctor said it probably wasn't a physical injury but likely something viral, I felt better about myself. I was stupid. She referred me to a rheumatologist.

"You have rheumatoid arthritis," he said. He was about my age and had an earnestness I liked. He explained that it was an autoimmune disease which meant that part of my body was striving to kick the shit out of other parts. It was common in women and the elderly. I looked at my watch and thought that was kind of bad luck.

"We'll start you on steroids and DMARD's, disease modifying antirheumatic drugs."

"Great. I can bulk up."

"Not those kinds of steroids." He didn't look up from his prescription pad.

I knew I should ask some questions; what are the effects of the drugs, what to expect, etc. I was young and an athlete. Between wrestling, skiing, rock climbing, mountain biking and assorted "Hey, watch this" moments, I had broken most of my body at one point or another. I shrugged.

"Are you allergic to codeine?" he asked. I shook my head, and he wrote another prescription. I didn't realize that the day before was the last day of my life that I didn't take a medication.

"We'll start with this and move to stronger painkillers when we need to." That seemed a little ominous. I looked at him more closely. He had a wedding band and wore gold cufflinks on his shirt. I usually didn't like guys who wore cufflinks.

RA was an insidious disease. It didn't kill. It stole. It stole mobility, self-reliance and self-respect. It had all the time in the world. I didn't wake up one day deformed and crippled. Instead, one morning I found that my thumb wouldn't straighten all the way. Several years later, the bones in my wrists were fused and tasks like brushing my teeth or wiping my ass became difficult. I started with a lean climber's physique and the strength to do two fingered pull ups. Somewhere along the way I started buying slip on shoes. I wrapped my hand in an ace bandage and claimed some injury to avoid the pain of handshakes; always reluctant to explain the disease. Eventually, I reached resignation and just handed the water bottle to my son to open for me.

There were many meds. Every day, week and month for the past twelve years I took a pill, gave myself a shot or was hooked up to an intravenous feed. That part never bothered me although it really grossed out the kids when they saw me jab a needle in my gut. When the first drug stopped working I knew there were many more. With the failure of the seventh or eighth one came the acute recognition that it was a war of attrition.

Bitterness ensued.

One drug, Remicade, required an IV that took a few hours. Once a month or so, I would sit in a room with a bunch of crippled old ladies, and we'd get our cocktail pumped into us. I was the novelty in the group, and they took great interest in my work, my kids, and my life. Given I was thirty or forty years younger than most of them, I willfully tried to avoid thinking what my condition would be at their age. I was afraid of them; gnarled old crones cackling as their blood was modified. Yes, I hated little old ladies who were in pain.

You could buy a pretty nice car every year for the cost of the newer drugs, called things like Humira or Orencia. Without insurance, it's impossible for most people to afford them. So, in November of last year I went off the good drugs.

• • •

I hobbled away from Greymoor the next morning. There was still pain, and getting my boot on had required inventive uses of the word "fuck", but I was functional. I waved to the circus guys and aimed toward another white blaze. It was a clear sky day and already warm even though the sun had just jumped the horizon. There were worse things than walking into the woods; even if it was with a limp.

I moved slowly, but I didn't have anywhere I needed to be. I smiled at that. I chewed on a granola bar as I went, and a couple squirrels soon fell in behind me to gather the crumbs. We moved along, and I was thankful for a long, gradual descent. I was the leader of squirrels. Their loyalty ceased as soon as the crumbs stopped falling, and I was again alone.

After a couple miles, I was regaining my sense of distance and no longer relied on the GPS, I came upon an old couple. He had a daypack, grey wool socks with a red stripe at the top pulled up to his knees, and big leather boots. She had a walker with tennis balls on the bottom of each of its legs.

"Good morning," she said as I approached. She said it with glee.

"Morning."

"You through hiking?" he asked.

"No, sir. Just section hiking." I looked at her twisted, ravaged legs.

"Beautiful day today," she said. She pulled off her floppy brimmed hat and lifted her face to the sun.

"You're going to get a sunburn," he said.

"I am not."

"You drive me crazy at times."

"I hope so." She winked at me.

"Have a good hike," I said and began to move on.

"You as well, young man," she called after me.

Would that be the BSW and me in a few years? Only I'd have the walker. That was a depressing thought.

• • •

I met her in a bar in East Greenwich, Rhode Island. I was a half hour early because I was still getting lost finding my way around that place, but that time I didn't. She later told me it annoyed her to find me already there because she was always early. She had come from the northern part of the state but assured me she didn't need to pack a lunch for the half hour drive. I didn't get the joke about Rhode Islanders' frame of reference for distance until she explained it to me. She ordered a good beer. Her hair was a short, tomboyish cut, and her elegantly manicured nails contrasted with her sturdy, strong hands.

I had fallen in love just a few times in my life. Each time was swift and certain, and I had an inkling that first meeting. Our second date I invited her to my place in what I wanted to be an impromptu, "Gosh, I made too much jambalaya. Want to come over and watch a movie?" sort of way. I didn't really think the plan through. My only television was in my bedroom. She seemed perfectly fine jumping on the bed and propping her head up with her hands. I sat on the edge and watched her butt more than the movie; well aware that, even though I was middle aged and divorced, women still scared the crap out of me.

On our third date she took me to a Brazilian steakhouse where we ate meat on swords on an outdoor patio. It was a beautiful, sunny evening, and I called her a beautiful, sunny woman, and she's been my BSW ever since. Then she took me back to her place on so many twisting, turning back roads that I considered if I were wrong about her, nobody would ever find my body. We talked for hours each night trying to catch up to the present in each other's lives. That was a couple weeks.

"Um, have you ever broken a bone?" she asked.

"Yes, most of them."

"Really?"

"Both legs, an ankle, all my fingers, most of my toes, an arm, some ribs, the nose, and a collarbone."

"You may want to stay indoors."

"Have you ever skydived?" I asked.

So it went.

We were in a coffee shop in downtown Providence. It was a funky place where hipsters in skinny pants typed on Macs and went outside to smoke clove cigarettes. We had already laughed about our presence ruining the place's cred. I had known her for three weeks. Amid the musky smell of the coffee beans, I knew, and it scared the holy, living shit out of me. I expressed as much to her and told her I was afraid and fragile. It sounded completely lame in hindsight, but I had several psychologists to vouch for me. She laughed at me and said, "You're not. You've just been listening to the people telling you that you are." Fortunately, she said she loved me too.

We went through the normal events of people who come to a relationship with some experience in life. I met her kids. In the summer she met my younger ones. Duncan decided she looked like an elf and called her Jingle. We spent a drunken weekend on Martha's Vineyard where we gave names and backstories to the people we encountered. I think we'd seen it in a Woody Allen movie. It became a favorite entertainment. At the end, we had a pantheon that included Bus Stop Guy, Annoying Neighbor, the Pope, and Buddy Holly. We went to St. Louis for my best friend's wedding to a guy nobody liked. We worked quickly to fill in the gaps in the half a life each of us had lived without the other. It did not take her long to know me better than anyone. She still stuck around.

For my part, I learned she liked shells and rocks and most animals more than most people. Her whimsy was well balanced by a sturdy New England practicality. Never give her a problem if you didn't want it solved. She delighted in pumpkins and catching raindrops on her tongue. I grudgingly admitted she was smarter than I in nearly all regards. She agreed. My need for open deserts was countered by hers for thick ocean air.

She told me we had fights, but I didn't remember them. My idea of a fight included saying a lot of intentionally hurtful things, shit got broken, and somebody stormed out of the house for a few days. We didn't have those.

She understood why I was out meandering probably better than I did.

• • •

I sat on the side of a rural road somewhere near the New York and New Jersey state line. That morning I had watched a bear eating wild blueberries, and it seemed incongruous how near I was to one of the largest cities on the planet. She was coming to resupply me and, I'm sure, assess for herself how I was doing. I had asked her to bring a camp stove, refills of my scripts, new socks and underwear. My diet of granola, energy bars and cold tuna was getting old.

Her green Jeep pulled up, and Bailey bounded out. He stopped and growled at me before recognition set in. Then I was slathered in Labrador kisses. I climbed in the Jeep and just like that had reentered civilization.

The air conditioning was cold, and the stereo was loud. It was strange to be in a car, disconcerting. I looked out the window at the receding trees.

We checked into a motel and walked around a small town; my pinky finger wrapped around her index finger. In a small pub, she sipped a Guinness and read my journal. I drank three beers, two glasses of ice water, and ate a cheeseburger, every fragment of French fry, and even the obligatory pickle slice on the plate. She paid.

"Your walk is helping," she said.

"Is it?"

"You seem slightly less fucked up."

"Thank you dear."

We spent the afternoon on a park bench making up stories for the people who passed. A man in a suit with his tie loosened became a guy who was caught cooking the books and was on his way to get a drink before going home to tell his wife they had to skip town. A woman pushing an old lady in a wheelchair was the granddaughter who hoped her attention to the old hag would ensure her place in the will. A young man with a faux hawk and a book bag hurried by and became a brilliant but unstable scientist on his way to his lab to confirm that the cure for cancer he had dreamt was real.

"You're very beautiful," I said.

"Are you on Percocet?"

"Not at the moment."

I put my arm around her. A little girl with pigtails was feeding geese. She approached a goose, threw a piece of bread, and ran squealing back to her mom.

That night, with Bailey sprawled snoring across the bottom of the bed, the BSW fell asleep with her head in my lap. I stroked her hair and brushed it back behind her ear. She hated that, but she was asleep, and I liked doing it. I stayed up late, which is to say until about ten, watching television. It had only been a couple weeks, but it seemed a novelty.

The next morning she drove me twenty miles south so I could bypass the great swamp. I was struck by the fact that the half hour drive would have been at least a full day's hike. My frame of reference was changing.

"So, you just walk into the woods?"

"Yeah. Pretty much." I put my hand on hers, and we sat there for a few minutes.

"Be careful," she said.

"Always."

"Yeah right. You know I love you."

"I love you." I kissed her. It was a long kiss; a kiss for remembering.

It was an inconsequential moment for her, it seemed; as if she was dropping me off at the airport for a business trip and would see me again in a few days. From the shadows of some trees at the wood line, I watched her drive away. Bailey had left nose prints on the windows, and there was a ding in her rear quarter panel. I lingered for a few minutes and looked at the road after she had driven out of sight. I walked away.

. . .

So, I met a porcupine. It was larger than I expected; about the size of a beagle. From our proximity, I could see that its quills looked nasty. They were dark, tapering to white points to give him a frosted appearance. He waddled as one might expect a man with a heavy pack and wet shorts to do. As I peered out at him in the early morning light, he shuffled to my underwear which I had hung under the rain fly to air out overnight. I had read they like the salt from our sweat.

What I had not read was what to do when meeting a porcupine. I knew with grizzlies to play dead and pray. I knew with black bears to look big and menacing. I knew with coyotes to make lots of noise and to walk widely around rattlers. I did not know what to do with a porcupine. My food was hanging in a tree to avoid attracting bears. It had not occurred to me that I needed to run my drawers up a flagpole.

My stick was perched against a tree beyond the porcupine. The spears on its back did not incline me to threaten violence any way. It seemed content snuffling my shorts. While I knew it was an herbivore, I was concerned it might take an interest in the source of salt. I did not want to start my day getting licked up by a porcupine.

So, I watched him from behind the mesh of the tent's bug door. He paid little attention to me except to occasionally turn a small dark eye toward me with a look I took to mean, "Bitch, I'm out here violating your underwear." Eventually, when my shorts had no crotch, he shook and dropped a few quills, and he waddled away. I picked one up and stuck it in the brim of my hat.

It had rained hard during the night, and the forest was still dripping. I duct taped my toes, chewed on a mint chocolate energy bar and prepared to get on with the business of hiking. I aimed my morning piss in the general direction the porcupine had gone and checked the color. Not wanting to litter the forest with a pair of crotchless, porcupine violated underwear, I stuffed them in the pack. I could see blue sky up through the canopy so I didn't put the rain cover on the pack.

It was slow going that morning. Place skin, shorts and a pack next to each other and add a little liquid, and you got friction to remove barnacles. However, put leaves on rocks and add a little rainwater, and you got a super slide. I slogged cautiously along thinking about the BSW and television. Each fern I passed shared some of the rain it held, and I quickly had soaked gaiters, socks, boots and sloshing feet. I wasn't sure there was room on my feet to add any new blisters so I just kept walking. A dry stream bed I had crossed several times the day before, our paths winding in the same general direction, was now running with drainage from the surrounding hills.

Crossing the stream again, I stepped on a rock without testing its stability. As soon as my weight descended on the rock, I knew it wasn't going to end well. The rock rolled. I windmilled the air for a moment then fell with a resounding thud onto my back in the stream. The pack cushioned the impact and kept my upper body above the few inches of runoff that was flowing. I lay there for a moment taking inventory of the body parts and decided nothing new was broken. My porcupine quill floated away.

In a clearing at least partially dried by the sun, I emptied the pack. The contents had received a lot more water than from just a seeping bladder. The guidebook, maps, notebook and journal, in their zip loc bags, were good. The sea grass rope was still tied to a compression strap. The down sleeping bag was a sopping brick. I wrung out my clothes and hung them on branches. The GPS and phone seemed to be okay. The BSW's laptop was the casualty. Its water proof bag apparently wasn't, and the screen was cracked. It had taken the bullet, and that sucked. I had been using the notebook more than the laptop any way, but it was one more thing I owed her.

I should have packed it out and disposed of it properly. Instead, I flung it like a Frisbee. It might have been more satisfying if it had exploded on impact. It just landed inconsequentially in a pile of leaves. That evening I got a fire going and strung lines above it. It hadn't taken long for the hiker stench to return, and the dousing eradicated some of that although it was replaced by pine smoke. The next morning when everything was thoroughly dried and smoked, I found the pack noticeably lighter in the absence of the laptop. I knew how hikers obsessed about weight, but I had been sure I needed everything I hauled.

At a dumpster in Bear Mountain Park, I began to shed. I tossed the pair of long pants I had yet to wear. Out went the bottle of biodegradable soap. Since I was traveling south, I ripped out the guidebook pages from Connecticut north. I discarded the camping pillow. I condensed the meds into a single bottle. The GPS had cost a lot. I held it in my hand and estimated its weight. Then, I left it and all my change on a picnic table. It was the first of several purges. Eventually, with an anorexic's need, I would saw off the handle of my toothbrush.

• • •

I was forty four years old. I had three or four children. I didn't know the correct way to answer that any more. At one time I had a mortgage and a home in the suburbs and a job that had "Vice President" in the title. Now I was sitting in a forest somewhere in New Jersey, and my net worth was substantially into the negative five figures.

So, I lost my job. My boss and the owner of the company hemmed and hawed. I wasn't sure they'd ever fired anyone; instead relying on people like me to do such things for them. After an hour of them explaining, I almost wanted to help them and instruct that these events were best done quickly with as little said as possible. I had gathered I was mostly being fired for chewing tobacco in meetings and using an almost profanity for my fantasy football team. I had taken a picture of a store's sign in Manhattan. It was "Fcuk," and I used it for my logo. I wanted to say I also didn't own any argyle socks or madras shorts.

To make themselves feel better, they then moved on to telling me of the many good things I had done. The year before I had been given a ten percent raise because of my performance. If not for the part about being fired, I would have almost hoped for another raise. Eventually, they felt good enough about themselves, and I was escorted to my office to pack my shit. The owner looked pleased about how things had gone. He had a son. For just a quick moment, I had a dark thought that might let him better understand me. Then I looked at the floor and walked out the door.

It was the Monday before Thanksgiving. A psychiatrist later pointed out to me that November sucks, at least for me. I never liked the job. I liked the paycheck though. I emailed my ex-wife to warn her that the checks that arrived every two weeks would be substantially smaller. Duncan, the younger of my sons, emailed back, "Why do you have to ruin everything?"

• • •

Pennsylvania had rocks. It was a land tilled by long departed glaciers. Every rock ever discovered, or to be discovered, was in Pennsylvania. Someone piled them all on the Appalachian Trail, creating one hundred some odd miles of hopscotch. One hiker I met wondered aloud why they had to put the trail on the rocky part as opposed to what appeared to be pristine forest floor around us. I considered explaining impact and erosion then decided to let him believe the trailblazers were so skilled and diabolical that they found this swath of rocks, marked it with white paint and called it a trail.

I paced along through a jumbled boulder field so thick there was no ground. There were just cracks that led down to other boulders. One chunk of granite, the size of a Volkswagen, barely balanced on the rock beneath and rolled like a teeter totter as I crossed. When I was a young man, bushwhacking up to climbing crags in Little Cottonwood canyon, I had been nimble and careless, leaping from rock to rock and across crevices. I walked cautiously among the rocks in Pennsylvania.

I almost died once in Little Cottonwood canyon. Sellers and I had our eye on a pitch called the Coffin. It was a high exposure face capped by a ten foot overhanging piece of granite. It was unbolted back then, and neither of us could lead the route. We came up with the brilliant idea of hiking up and around, dropping ropes, and then toproping the climb. It was a good plan except for attempting something significantly beyond our capabilities. That's what my dad said. I thought it was a good plan except for an underestimation of rope length. And the part when I almost died.

I scrambled my way up through the scree to the side and hedged my way over until I was above the Coffin. A stunted Pinon pine growing out of the rock there made for a solid rappel point. From the bottom looking up, we had seen that there was a belay sling set in the nook where the coffin rock emerged at a near right angle from the rising cliff face. I would rappel down over the rock, tie into that sling, and drop another rope to the ground.

I stuck my butt out into the air and began to batman down. It went fine until I went over the upper edge of the coffin. Swinging in the breeze a hundred or so feet above the ground, I came literally to the end of my rope. I was dangling ten feet away from the cliff face. I did not have enough rope left to swing my way in to the belay. With my weight on the rope it was too taut for me to go back up over the edge. So, I swung there grinning. Sellers was on the ground yelling at me.

I could have hung there until he followed my route up and tossed down a longer rope from the Pinon, but I didn't. I started rocking until I was swinging long arcs in the sky and the cliff face was coming within just a couple feet of my outstretched hand. Then I released my rappel hand and the last bit of rope slipped out of my harness. For an instant that seemed like frozen time, I was connected to neither rope nor rock. I slammed into the cliff and grabbed the sling. I dislocated two fingers. With my good hand I clipped in to the sling and waited for the sewing machine action of my leg to subside, a product of adrenaline overload. I saw the sparkling flecks in the granite reflecting sunlight. A hawk rode the thermals in the canyon below me. In the distance I could see the smog of Salt Lake City's suburbs. It was spectacular.

A few years ago Sellers stuck a gun in his mouth and pulled the trigger. He left behind three children from his three ex-wives.

The AT in Pennsylvania mostly traverses ridgelines. In other places, the spaces between ridges are called valleys or hollows. In that place they're called gaps. Gut busting climbs up and knee crushing descents to the gaps are interspersed with miles and miles of horizontal trudging through the rocks. The ridge I was on was relatively small. I could see from the topo that it was maybe four miles long, a mile or so wide and rose a little over four hundred feet from its surrounding low points. I was sure the locals called it something, but the map did not give it a name. That bothered me.

I decided I would know that anonymous fin. Instead of just passing over its back and moving on to new country, I would become deeply aware of that little corner of the world. I walked its perimeter: a winding highway on two sides with a clogged zone of discarded soda bottles and hamburger wrappers, a junkyard with skeletons of cars on another, and an empty dirt road at the southern end. I walked up gullies and down ravines. I saw deer, crows, toads and a bull snake that called it home. I found a rusty screwdriver with a rotting wooden handle.

I spent three days on that hill. For a time, the need to keep moving ebbed. I watched the sun rise over distant green hills then I walked across the ridge and watched it set among different green hills. Following faint game trails, or no trails at all, I saw no people. It had been twenty years, back in dusty deserts, since I had gone twenty four hours without seeing another person. I touched thistles and milkweed and walked through a meadow of vivid blue lupines. I was repeatedly caught and released by a vicious thorny vine I could not name. I napped beneath a massive rhododendron and shared an energy bar with sparrows and grackles.

On the second day I discovered a spring. On my hands and knees, I was following a toad. It was a plump little guy with dark brown markings. He didn't seem to mind my company; taking small hops then watching me with a rolling eye while I crawled to catch up. I named him Guido and asked him aloud where we were heading. After some time, Guido led me onto damp soil. It held just a faint hint of moisture, and I would not have noticed if I were not on my belly trying to get eye to eye with a toad.

I crawled up the hill tracking by the feel of the dirt until I could smell the water. Beneath a peeling birch, water seeped from an outcropping of rock. Deer tracks filled in the mud below, and I debated disturbing the place. It was more proximate than the three mile round trip to a stream at the bottom of the northern gap. I built a small ring of stones, filled the joints with mud, lined the bottom with rocks, and I had a dipping pool. Hikers said dipping pool, I think, because it sounded more appealing than puddle. Belying the water that barely seemed to ooze from the rocks, the pool filled pretty quickly.

Compass in hand, counting my steps and wishing the GPS still belonged to me, I walked due West up the hill until I reached the ridgeline and the trail. I turned around frequently to remember the view on the return. I built a small rock cairn to mark the spot then went to my camp to get the water filter and a bladder. A couple toads were enjoying the dipping pool when I returned. Guido wasn't one of them. I sat nearby for a while and enjoyed the coolness the evaporation created in the forest.

The urge to move, to evade, returned. When I finally left my hill I felt that, even if I did not know all its secrets, I knew it well enough. I had honored that place that was just one more hill that hikers crossed and locals drove around. The hill was not inconsequential. Back on the trail, I descended into the southern gap. When I reached the dirt road at the bottom I would be traveling new ground again. I ran into two NoBo's working their way up out of the gap.

"How's the water ahead?" One of them asked.

"There's a stream still flowing at the northern gap, and there's a spring up off the ridgeline. The next shelter is dry."

"There's no spring in the guide book," the other said.

"It's there. It's called Guido Spring," and I gave them directions. I was pleased.

• • •

I didn't remember the events that got me strapped to a bed in a sterile white room. I did remember being incoherently outraged to learn that they could in fact keep me there. I was later told that I ranted well into the night; verbally lashing at anyone that ventured in. Amid profanities I asked the security guard if it required a GED to do his job. I screamed at an orderly that, given why I was there, I probably didn't give a fuck about his opinion. Chalk up another fine moment for me. In hindsight, I always felt worse about things I said that night than the act that got me there. At some point I was loaded into another ambulance and woke the next day locked in the nut wing of a downtown Denver hospital.

Even by hospital standards, it was an austere and stark place. There were no cheap prints on the walls. The nurse's station was a secure room with wire in its windows, and everything was painted a sort of beige color. Perhaps it was meant to be more soothing than sanitized white to the inhabitants' troubled minds. It somehow seemed less clean; a commentary on the patients it served.

I learned that, when you try to kill yourself, they can legally keep you for up to seventy two hours. I was locked away with crashing drug addicts, other suicide failures, and complete psychos. I wondered, without irony, why I was the only normal person who tried to kill himself. After a lifetime of successes, I had failed at marriage and suicide in the same year. I laughed at that and quickly learned that breaking into bitter laughter for no apparent reason did not help one's cause in that place.

I took too many or not enough pills, depending on perspective, on the evening of December twenty second. My seventy two hours of lockdown would include Christmas day. Not rationally recognizing that being dead would have put quite a damper on Christmas for my kids, I did not want to ruin the holiday because daddy was locked in the nut house.

So, my entire focus came to be getting out. My assigned psychiatrist was Dr. Frankenfucker. I didn't remember his real name. He was arrogant and disdainful and wore cufflinks, and I later learned he slept with a patient. Thankfully, it wasn't me. I desperately wanted to tell him that, amid the man who screamed at his dead wife all night, the young girl with bandages on her wrists who went round the ward asking people to fuck her, and my roommate who carried on conversations with himself in the dark, nobody was getting better in that hell. Instead, I told him whatever he wanted to hear. I shared in group therapy; making up events from my childhood. I played self-esteem bingo and colored pictures. I did puzzles with schizophrenics and made up shit about how it taught me coping strategies. The real lesson I learned was don't do puzzles with schizophrenics. The nurses smiled and told me what great progress I was making. By the end of the second day I was even allowed a razor to shave. They were rightfully cautious with sharp objects in that place. Dr. Frankenfucker was tougher to persuade.

In a "scared straight" video produced for fourteen year olds, I also learned that killing oneself is surprisingly difficult. Overdosing required a lot more pills than one would expect. If you did manage to take enough, there was a very good chance that the body's natural defense mechanisms would kick in, and you'd puke them all out. When I later heard about some celebrity dying from accidental overdose, I was kind of morbidly impressed. There was also a good chance of not dying, at least initially, even if the pills stayed down. Instead, one got organ failure. The quick, painless death envisioned instead became an agonizing deathmarch. Contrary to the theme from *MASH*, suicide was not painless.

"The food here sucks." She said it in such a way that it seemed open for discussion and that she had a frame of reference on the quality of food in such places. I stabbed at my own meat product in gravy with my plastic fork and did my best to hope she wasn't talking to me. Even though I was the only other person in the room, in that place it wasn't a certainty.

"I said the food here sucks." She said again and poked at the air with her fork. I looked up at the bandages on her wrists. She was younger than my daughter, and half of her blue hair was shaved.

"Yeah, it does," I said. She glared at me, and I guessed she hadn't been talking to me at all.

"I cut myself," she said and held up both bandaged wrists for me to see. "Again."

"I OD'ed," I said. What had happened in her young life that she was here for at least the second time? An image of my daughter Quinn bandaged and locked up there pushed into my head.

"No, you didn't," she said.

She had a point. The nurse came and collected our plates and plastic utensils. As I was leaving, I heard the girl behind me.

"Wanna fuck me?"

I cringed and thought of Quinn again and felt a renewed shame for being there.

I spent Christmas Eve eating processed turkey loaf and watching *It's a Wonderful Life* with all the other nut jobs.

Dr. Frankenfucker released me on Christmas morning after I promised to enroll in an outpatient psychiatric program first thing Monday morning. Perhaps he knew there was no way I was ever stepping foot in that building again. His parting fuck you to me was that he would only release me to the woman with whom I was in the middle of a bitter divorce proceeding. That was not a pleasant car ride.

In the few years since, I thought of suicide many times. A significant deterrent was not death but fear of another failure; that I would end up in that place again.

• • •

A paper plate was tacked to a tree. I was still in Pennsylvania and still navigating seas of rock. Handwriting on the plate said, "Trail Magic ahead." A while later I passed another paper plate sign that read, "This is your lucky day." Trail magic was random acts of kindness. Those who provided the magic were called angels. It was as simple but important as jugs of water. It was sometimes delightful or whimsical. One day I came across a bucket of sliced watermelon in the forest. On another, I found a Styrofoam cooler of beer and ibuprofen tablets. That lukewarm PBR, drank while sitting in the dust, was one of the best beers I ever had. With that billboard buildup, I was hoping for something extravagant like those peanut butter cheese crackers or maybe sodas. Magic was usually left where the trail crossed a road. Placed just a few yards into the forest, it was rarely discovered by anyone except hikers. This place was miles from the next road crossing. I passed another sign that said, "You're almost there."

I crested a small rise and walked into what appeared to be a cook out. A group of people, maybe six or seven which was a large collection out there, seemed to be waiting just for me. They helped me off with my pack, and a guy handed me a cup of Gatorade that he never let get empty. I was offered a seat on a stump. One man strummed a guitar while another tended hot dogs on a grill over a fire. I was slightly bewildered.

We traded trail names, talked about the weather, and I learned that two of them had through hiked and all had done significant sections. I munched on chili dogs with cheese and onions.

"We're a long ways from the road," I said. I was looking at the mountain of food they had.

"It was quite a haul," said the man cooking the dogs.

"Yeah it was," said another.

"All you packed were the chips," said the guitar player. My cup was filled again. I ate another chili dog and thought about eating hotdogs with my dad at baseball games. I always liked those times.

"This is amazing," I said.

"It's our way of giving back to the trail," said the cook.

"Here comes the sermon," the guitar player said. The cook threw a hotdog at him.

"Run, Polar!"

I ate and drank until I could hold no more. They continued their banter. As I prepared to leave I was given enough granola bars and peanut butter cheese crackers to stuff my cargo pockets.

"Thank you very much," I said.

"Thank you," the cook said. He grinned.

"For what?"

"For hiking."

I shook hands all around and turned down the trail. I could hear their laughter carry through the forest for a little while. Then, I was again walking alone. What had the trail given them that prompted their generosity? I passed a Canada Lily near the trail. The yellow flowers were too heavy for their stems and had tipped over to point at the ground. Could I find something like that glee on the trail? I picked a flower and sniffed it as I walked, and then I tossed it aside.

. . .

There were things I did not know. Okay, there were lots of things I didn't know. I had a complete lack of knowledge about brain surgery, astrophysics, or the popularity of watching golf on television. I didn't understand how cell phones worked or why laundry needed to be separated. I used to think I understood women. Then I got married. Then I got divorced. When I was a teenager, my father would say, "Leave home now while you still know everything." Perhaps whatever wisdom we gained with age was just recognition of ignorance.

I had passed an old growth oak tree. It was about three feet across at its base, and its crown was far above its neighbors'. I had seen few old trees so far. The forests were filled with trunks barely a foot wide or smaller. Was it logging or disease or something else?

I didn't know.

I spent a morning hiking and considering things I did not know. Why weren't there more old trees in the forests? What was the bug that had evolved for the sole purpose of flying into my eyeball and dying? How did the spiders know to build their webs at face height? I did not know the name of the brown centipede that grew to be the size of a man's thumb and seemed to be a buffet for every other bug in the forest. I could not name enough of the birds I saw. I could confirm however, through personal witness, the answer to the rhetorical question of bears shitting in the woods. I did not know enough about butterflies.

Actually, I knew almost nothing about butterflies. I could identify a Monarch, and I realized that was the only butterfly I could name. I saw flocks of small yellow ones hovering like lemon colored clouds. I had to call them lemon cloud butterflies. I had seen, on occasion, an achingly beautiful butterfly that started bright sky blue and faded to deep inky darkness. It was like twilight captured on a wing. I felt I should know its name; that there might be some important distinction to be made between people who could name butterflies and those who could not.

I walked ten miles before noon thinking mostly about butterflies and old trees, and I again emerged from the forest. It had been a while since a shower or clean underwear so I was aiming for a state park campground a couple miles off the trail. I had gone just a little way down the road when a car coming toward me veered onto the shoulder. I thought initially he was running me off the road. It had happened before. I picked up a rock to throw.

The car pulled up beside me, and the driver, an obese guy said, "Get in. I'll give you a ride."

"I'm good. Thanks."

"I always hated having to do any walking off the trail." A car behind him was already honking. He might not have been a butterfly guy, but he at least knew hikers. I shoved my pack and stick in the back seat and climbed in. There were assorted fast food bags on the floor and a bunch of bird feathers in a cup holder between us. The car smelled like body odor and French fries.

I learned his name was Phil. He had thick varicose veins bulging on his legs. He had been a hiker before surgery. He knew a lot of hikers headed for the campground so he cruised the highway to give rides.

"That's nice," I said.

He dropped me at the campground office and offered to come by in the evening to give me a ride into town. I thanked him and declined. I hurried into the office.

Phil was not a butterfly guy.

In a camp spot built to hold a motor home, I planted my one person tent. A log building a hundred yards away had toilets that flushed, toilet paper, and lukewarm showers. I washed myself and all my clothes with a bar of soap someone had left behind. After repeated scrubbings, the hiker stench seemed to be gone. In sopping shorts and t-shirt, I strung the rest up in the pines between my spot and the circus sized tent in the next one over. It was still early afternoon so I walked down to the lake, dripping all the way. At the camp store I bought a can of salmon, a pepperoni stick, some vegetable soup and a chocolate bar. I ate my chocolate and watched the people stay carefully within the designated swimming area which was marked by large pink buoys. When the chocolate was gone, I aimed back toward my camp spot and shook my head about pink buoys.

Dinner was coming along nicely. I had boiled an energy drink down to a thick syrup. The soup was strained off, and the little cubed vegetables were spread on a rock next to the fire. The sliced pepperoni was on another rock. The salmon was wrapped in the pepperoni's foil container in the coals. I missed my kitchen. A girl and boy, maybe five and seven, and each wearing North Face sweatshirts in corresponding pink and blue, came to visit from the circus tent next door.

"Hi," I said.

"Where's your car?" the girl asked.

I smiled and said, "I left it at home." It might have been repossessed at that point. Their parents hurried over. He was carrying a fried chicken leg.

"I'm sorry," said the mother.

"Quite a rig you have," the father said and smiled. It was more of a smirk.

"It does the job." I looked him in the eye and smirked right back.

The mother asked if I was hiking the trail then explained to her husband and the children what it was. The little girl asked how far I had walked.

"What do you eat out there?" the father asked.

"A couple hundred miles. Tonight its smoked salmon in a berry reduction with stone fired pepperoni crisps and roasted vegetables." I had done some menu design in my career. I smirked some more. He ushered his family back to their neck of the woods. The mother wished me well on my hike. I looked at the size of their tent and thought of pink buoys. That wasn't camping. The little girl brought me a s'more later on.

By evening, the campground bustled like a small city. Kids went by on bikes. A ranger made his rounds in a golf cart. An old couple took a stroll and chatted with the neighbors. I watched a guy spend twenty minutes backing up his camp trailer while his wife sat at a picnic table talking on her cell phone. I went in my tent, but it did not block the sounds of cars and shouts and the stereo playing Rolling Stones songs.

I went back down to the lake. A chain was strung across the paved path with a sign saying the beach was closed. I climbed over it. The lake was quiet and reflected the rising slice of moon. Here and there it rippled in rings as fish rose for dinner. I stripped down and waded in. I swam out and dived under the line on the pink buoy. Behind me, campfires, lanterns and the lights from recreational vehicles glowed through the trees. Ahead, there was the moon and the first stars. I wished I were a stronger swimmer and returned to the shore.

• • •

Another hiker had come in while I was swimming. He was set up in the spot on the other side of mine. Our little tents looked funny in lots the size of basketball courts. I sat on my picnic table to see what stars I could through the ambient light, and he came over to say hello. He was a young guy with shaggy brown hair and wisps of a beard. He reminded me a little of Keegan, my older son, and I looked at him with a sad smile. He bummed a dip off me, and we sat there spitting into the dirt.

He called himself Ajax and told me he was "going all the way," and tomorrow was his first zero day in three weeks. We talked about when he thought he'd reach Katahdin, how he'd built his own alcohol burning stove with a beer can, and the availability of water in both directions. At one point he commented on the smell of barbecue in the air, and I told him the camp store sold burgers and dogs.

"AT on a budget, man. I've been eatin' nothing but ramen and power bars for months." He explained how he'd mailed boxes of noodles and energy bars to post offices up the trail. Every ten days or so, he went off the trail to collect his rations. That was something Keegan would have done.

A couple girls walked past, and his attention was diverted. He asked for another dip, told me to have a great hike, and went to talk to them. I looked up to try to find Orion in the sky.

I was sipping my instant coffee and watching the forest wake up the next morning when an alarm clock went off in the circus tent at six o'clock. The father swore, and the alarm was turned off. I hoisted my pack; determined to get out of campground city before it came alive. Ajax was snoring. I paused and lowered my pack and dug out my notebook. I wrote

"Have a cheeseburger. Stay away from Phil" and wrapped the page around a ten dollar bill. I weighted it down with a rock near the entrance to his tent.

I walked up the highway thinking about my son and hoped Phil wasn't an early riser.

. . .

When the BSW caught me in the woods near our home with a bottle of painkillers, another of sleeping pills, and a six pack of beer, she demanded I get help. It wasn't a serious attempt; just contemplating the possibilities. Still, it skeeved her out.

"I'm not going to therapy," I said.

"There are different kinds of therapy."

"Tell me about your childhood. And how does that make you feel?"

"Shut up."

It was a nondescript building near a strip mall. A group of people smoked off to one side of the entrance. One was wearing a coat although it was eighty degrees. Another appeared to have only about three teeth. A man paced back and forth mumbling to himself. It was the place where those without recourse went for mental health assistance. I sighed. She squeezed my hand.

"This should be fun," I said.

"Think of it as utilizing your tax dollars."

"Let the healing begin."

I sat in a hard plastic chair and filled out forms and questionnaires.

Yes, I had suicidal thoughts.

No, I did not think of harming others.

No, I did not own a gun.

Yes, I drank frequently.

No, I did not use illegal drugs.

No, I did not abuse my pets.

Yes, I liked violent movies.

No, I did not hear voices.

Yes, I had previously been diagnosed with a mental disorder.

Yes to depression.

Yes to bipolar.

No to schizophrenia.

No, I did not wet the bed.

Yes, I had trouble sleeping.

No, I had not been convicted of a felony.

I thought about answering yes to every question just to see the response. I was interviewed by a case worker then we met with the psychiatrist.

She spoke with a strong eastern European accent. The BSW guessed Romania. It turned out she was from Transylvania. If I had to see a psychiatrist, and I had to do so at the state operated mental health clinic, how cool was it that she was from Transylvania?

"Why are you here today?" Dr. Dracula asked and looked at my forms.

"She made me," I replied and gestured toward the BSW.

"Do you think you need help?"

"Yes, but I'm doubtful you can provide it." I stared back as she appraised me.

"It is my job today to determine if it is safe for you to go home," she said.

"What?" I looked around the room to the closed door and the window with bars. The BSW held my hand.

She asked me many questions to ascertain my state of mind. We discussed my arthritis, my job loss, and my family. With the BSW there, I had to be honest in my responses. I kept my eye on the door.

"From what you've told me, I'm not inclined to think you're bipolar."

"Excellent."

"You do have severe clinical depression." I wanted to say "no shit", but I didn't.

"We have many programs."

"I'm not going to therapy," I interrupted her. We stared at each other again. The BSW explained I had a bad experience with therapy. I explained that I tried to kill myself the day after I saw my last therapist, and he billed me for the session I missed while I was locked up in the psych ward.

"Then we'll look at the medication options," she said. "You don't like that either?"

I guess my face betrayed me.

"You can't prescribe a pill that will change the events that make me unhappy, only my response to the events."

Then she lectured me that depression was an illness and that suicidal thoughts were not a rational or healthy response. I gathered she was not an existentialist. I considered debating, but I did want to go home.

Eventually I left with prescriptions for three varieties of happy pills and some sleepy pills and an appointment for the next week. And I diligently took them for a time.

· · ·

Hiking the Appalachian Trail was not an escape into solitude. It was an escape into a less populated world. I had been in a desert nine miles removed from the nearest rutted dirt road; that being sixteen miles from the nearest paved road and that being thirty miles removed from even a gas station. It took no effort to be alone in that place. I could count on my fingers the number of people I might see on a given day on the trail, but true solitude took a little work.

I found veering even a quarter mile off the trail helped. I spent some days hiking parallel to the trail but a few hundred yards removed. That also forced me to engage with my surroundings. Compass and map in hand, I paid attention to the contours of the land. A slight incline or decline meant something. As a degree of fitness had returned, my pack got lighter, and hiking stopped being painful, I found the markings on the trail to be like the white line fever of a highway. I could hike for miles and recall little I had passed.

Once I was eating lunch ten feet off the trail. I was sitting on a log, and my red pack was propped up next to me. I was wearing a blue shirt. Two hikers approached. They were lean and with the long beards of through hikers. Their arms worked their poles like pistons, and they stared down at the ground in front of them. They were moving at probably faster than three miles per hour. They never looked up. They never looked to the side. They did not see me. They would reach Katahdin, and it would be a great accomplishment. They might as well have spent five months on a treadmill.

They were on a mission. I was on a meander. There were days I pounded out twenty five or thirty miles. There were days I did not. One day I walked a couple hundred yards, spent most of the day chasing lizards through boulders, then went back to my previous camp spot because it had a nice view. More commonly, I went fifteen to twenty miles a day.

At their core, my days became a combination of traveling some distance and finding water. It was a short but critical to do list. Between bladders and bottle, I had the capacity to hold seven liters of water. That's a lot of weight. I typically hiked with three liters and would fill all the way up only if I knew it was going to be a dry camp or upcoming water sources were sketchy. I grew up in the desert so I paid close attention to water. Every morning I looked at the color of my piss. Bright yellow, smelly urine meant not enough water.

Summer marched on, and water became scarce. Streambeds were dusty, and springs were dry. Water was the primary topic of conversation among hikers, and log books were checked for status updates on water sources. Moving a body and its pack fifteen or twenty miles day in and out required a lot of fuel. I found I needed to drink about eight liters of water a day to have a good, clear piss in the morning. It wasn't a life or death situation like a man sprawled on a sand dune. A few liters of water will keep someone alive for quite a while. It was, though, critical to keeping the hike going. A lot of hikers just wore down, wore out, and quit from a prolonged water deficit.

The sun had raked the sky. The rocks beneath could cook pizzas. Even the trees felt warm to the touch. A thunderstorm had blasted through earlier. It didn't leave enough to be useful; just a swelter. I had hidden under a rhododendron during the cruelest hours.

I was at a shelter, and the guidebook said there were three springs down the hill. I had a quarter liter of water in my bottle. The shelter's log book showed the first spring was dry but the next two were flowing as of two days ago.

Four times that day I had made the long sweaty descent off the ridgeline looking for water. Four times I reached dry springs and made the long sweaty ascent back up with a dry mouth. I had been assured that one of the springs was running just the day before by another hiker. I actually gave that guy water. Asshole.

I dumped the pack and stripped off all weight that was not required for fetching water. It was a big ridge, seven hundred vertical feet to the bottom, and the closely bunched lines on the topographical map showed it was going to be a haul. I followed the blue blazes, used to mark side trails, down. I descended by hanging from tree branches and skidding through stones. Rocks I kicked loose tumbled until they disappeared in the trees.

I checked the first spring just to be sure. The second was dry too. I kept going to the bottom. I knew I would drink the last of the water I had just on the scramble back up to my pack. The last spring was capped with a pump at the base of the hill. It was in a small gravel parking lot on a dirt road that wasn't even on my map.

The pump handle creaked. I pumped. I pumped some more. I rested and pumped again. Only air moved with each heave of the iron handle. I sat down and looked at the map. As best I could tell it was about nine miles to civilization. Back up on the trail it was seven miles to the next spring. I sat there and thought about Guido the toad. The thunderstorm had left puddles in the ruts of the parking lot. Their oily sheen glistened in the final rays of sun.

The puddle was vile. There was a film of oil on it refracting colors, and it turned into a grey murk when I stirred it with my stick. It was eighteen miles roundtrip to a certain water source. It was seven miles to a roll of the dice. The puddle was wet. It was definitely not a dipping pool. I could see the knobby tire tracks under the water. I walked over to look down the gravel road.

It disappeared around a lonely bend.

I pumped it through my filter, added sterilizing drops then pumped it through the filter again. It didn't taste great, but it wasn't awful, and I drank a liter there. I thought I should probably google the filter's effectiveness on heavy metals, but the phone was up in the pack. I climbed up through the twilight with twenty pounds of water.

On the ridge it was still day time. A few hikers had come in to the shelter.

"Bet it's the last one," one said and laughed when I came up the trail with my water bladders.

"It's dry too."

He looked at me. "Then, where'd you get the water?"

"Puddle in a parking lot."

"That's gross," said the woman with them. I sat down and took a long drink.

"Is there more?" one asked.

One by one they each left to go down the hill. I loaded my pack and went to find a quiet and isolated place to camp. I wasn't really working so hard to stay alive. Returning to the world was what scared me.

• • •

Palmerton, PA was a superfund site. There was a ridgeline above Palmerton that was mined and stripped for zinc for over a hundred years. It looked like a nuclear bomb site. I walked along the dead ridge. Desiccated corpses of trees littered the hillside. I was the only living thing more than a foot tall. I hiked for miles through that wasteland. I was not surprised by our capacity for the rape of the earth, but I was still stunned being in the midst of its aftermath. I went as quietly as possible through the graveyard. Far below me the borough of Palmerton bustled. I wondered how often they glanced up at the dead mountain.

I descended through a cascade of rocks. All the soil had been blasted away. Boulders tumbled with my passage, and I slipped, clung and slid to the bottom; maybe carrying down some of the death or pushing it before me. At the bottom I met a new and live problem. The side trail into Palmerton, that paralleled the highway, was closed due to construction. The highway was a four lane screamer with a support wall right next to it.

I peered down the road. There was no option of waddling, or even sprinting, along. I could have just crossed and continued on my way, but I needed to resupply, and I wanted to see that town that killed a mountain. So, I stuck out my thumb. I had not hitchhiked since I was fifteen years old ditching class and catching a ride up the canyon to ski. The eighty seventh car stopped. It was an old man in an old truck.

"Get in!"

I threw my gear in the bed and hopped into the passenger seat. Cars jockeyed to get past him.

"Guess you want to go to the jail," he said.

I wasn't sure where I wanted to go, but I was pretty sure it wasn't the jail. I guess I was silent in my consideration long enough because he started to laugh.

"We converted our jail to a hostel. All the hikers go there. It's a great place. Hot showers, bunks, even have access to the basketball court."

Jail was sounding better.

He asked how far I'd hiked and where I was headed. I learned he was from Palmerton, had walked every hill within fifty miles, only left home when sent to Normandy in the big one, had raised three sons, one of them was in prison but the other two were respectable, and he still hated Bill Clinton.

He dropped me at the city hall, which in big block letters they called the BOROUGH HALL, wished me well, and he sped away after I barely managed to dig my pack out of his bed. He was off to meet his lady friend, as he called her. It was Friday at four p.m., and borough hall was preparing to close. I hurried in and approached the window. The receptionist smiled and slid a clipboard to me and asked for identification. I had to find my wallet down in the bottom of the pack. I was given a welcome bag with a map of Palmerton, coupons to local businesses, a toothbrush, a pen, and a granola bar. The borough manager gave me a tour and showed me how to unlock the crash bar on the basement door so I could come and go.

At five o' clock I was the only one in city hall.

The jail was a concrete room in the basement with bunk beds made from two by fours and plywood. There was a picnic table in the center. On a shelf were items left behind by other hikers. I rummaged through partially used fuel containers, open bags of rice with mouse droppings, packets of hot sauce and a few tent stakes; discarded things. The showers, upstairs off the gymnasium, blasted a jet of water, but they were hot. On my way back through the gym I picked up an errant basketball and took a shot. My towel fell off. How many can say they played naked basketball in city hall?

"I'm in jail," I said.

"What did you do?" the BSW asked.

I told her about Palmerton and she asked for a picture of me in jail. She said she'd been able to sell my bike, watch and kayaks. Once upon a time I had paid three grand for that watch in a shop on Fifth Avenue. I felt a little like Augie March in Mexico except I didn't have a rich brother or know any criminals to fall back on. Still, I had a very efficient BSW, and I was more liquid than I had been in some time. I called in to make my weekly unemployment claim.

The first batch of clothes came out of the dryer, and I went in the restroom to change. Clean underwear felt so good. With the dirty clothes swishing in the coin op washer, I went next door to the barbershop. It had an old fashioned red and white striped pole in front. Inside were jars of combs in astringent blue liquid. The barber shaved the hot lather off my face with a straight razor, wiping it on a towel across his shoulder as he went.

"Don't get too many hikers in here. They seem to like those beards," he said.

"I'm not a hiker."

He laughed.

I resupplied at the super market with packages of instant pasta, rice, foil envelopes of tuna and salmon, instant oatmeal, coffee, energy bars, a head of garlic and a can of spam. I took all my food to the butcher counter and asked them to weigh it. I planned to eat the spam the next day so I wouldn't have to carry it for long.

The library was having a book sale, and I picked up a paperback copy of *The Myth of Sisiphys*. When I asked the librarian how much she told me they were free for hikers. Showered, shaved, in clean clothes, I had even taken the bandana off my head, I wondered what it was that identified me. I walked along Main Street watching families push strollers, teenagers with skateboards hanging out, and couples holding hands. I had been each one of those at some point. Would I have felt as foreign if I had driven into town and checked into the hotel?

At the local tavern I sat at the end of the bar and splurged on a prime rib. I salivated waiting for it. I drank a couple Yuenglings while watching baseball on the television. I had run assorted errands. I was relaxing and having a beer. They were normal activities. I wanted them to be normal, but they felt strange, like things *those* people did.

"How many games back are the Phillies?" the guy next to me asked.

"Sorry, I don't know."

He looked at me.

"Where you hiking to?" he asked.

"Virginia." I had taken to making up a concrete answer to the question because saying I had no idea always led to more intimate questions.

I went back to jail and watched bugs die on the fluorescent light. My time in the trees was changing me.

• • •

The next morning I had eggs with scrapple and hash browns and several cups of strong, black coffee in a diner at the end of town. The waitress called every customer "honey." Then, I lifted my pack from by the door. Like a miner who had found a small nugget, I had come to town, but I was eager to return. I walked to where the highway began and stuck out my thumb. Early on a Saturday, there were few cars, and none stopped.

After an hour, the sun was getting on with its day, and I was getting annoyed. I walked down a side street to where the closed access trail was. There was a chain link fence across a bridge and several signs hung from it.

No trespassing.
Keep out.
Danger.

I hiked back to the diner and asked if there was a taxi in town. No taxi. I went to the police station with the idea that, by asking how to get to the trail, they might give me a ride. The police station was closed on Saturdays. I could feel anxiety creeping in, and I looked up first at the big dead mountain then south to the hill I was trying to get to. My heart beat faster. I needed to leave.

So, I went back to the access trail. The river that the bridge crossed looked too deep to wade. Barb wire on the top of the fence prevented me climbing it. The highway was just down the hill to the right. I slid down the embankment and looked at the highway's bridge across the river. It was about thirty yards long, two lanes wide, with no shoulder. It shook and swayed when the semi trucks thundered by. I watched for a few minutes. The sun was still climbing. I told myself I was losing daylight, but that was irrelevant.

I tightened up the straps on my pack and counted how long it took a truck to come into view and then reach the bridge. It was about nine seconds. I tried to do the math, but I couldn't focus. I looked down and saw my knuckles were white on my stick. I waited until the road was clear, and I ran, counting as I went. One, and I was on the bridge. Two, and I was running, building speed. Three, and a truck rounded the bend. Four, and he started to honk. I ran hard. I could hear his brakes screeching. I could see the Kenworth truck logo on his grill when I reached the other side and dove left. Gasping in the gravel, it occurred to me that would have been a quick way to go.

I scrambled up to the access trail. My hope was there would be nobody working on Saturday. I walked past bulldozers and backhoes and generators, but I did not see any people. There were rolls of thick wire mesh that they were bolting onto the mountain to keep rocks from falling on the highway. It looked like a skin graft. I hiked uneventfully the two miles back until I reached the point where it merged with the Appalachian Trail. There was another fence and signs across that end, but I just walked around that one.

On the other side was a small trailer, and a man came out wearing a yellow jacket with "security" printed on the back. He wanted to know what I was doing coming *from* the no trespassing zone. I said I was lost and just trying to get back on the trail; which was mostly true.

"I better call this in," he said as he surveyed me.

He pulled out a radio and turned his back to me. I considered the possible outcomes. At the very least it was going to take some time. At the worst I didn't want to visit Palmerton's real jail.

So, I walked away. The security guard yelled at me to stop, but I didn't look back. It was hot. He was fat. I didn't think he'd chase me. I'd just outrun a tractor trailer. After a couple hundred yards I stopped, changed into a different colored shirt and replaced my bandana with the wide brimmed floppy hat. I followed the trail down to the highway where I had hitched the day before. I waited for an opening in traffic and half expected a police car to come rushing around the curve with flashing lights and sirens. None came, and I crossed and passed, grinning, back into the wood line.

• • •

On some days I would follow the white blazes through the long green tunnel and just enjoyed that my mind could sometimes wander again and not get stuck in the dark. The bare roots of trees might first look like coiled snakes, then dragon's feet, then aliens that unfurled out of the walls; only to be driven away by songbirds with golden throats.

Another web across the face, with a spider dangling on its end, sparked a genre hopping epic.

"Woo hoo! I got one!" The spider said with a southern accent.

"Hang onto him. Steady. Reel him in."
"We can't hold him much longer, captain," this spider was Scottish.
"We need more power!" another spider said.
"Dammit, I'm a spider, not an engineer."
"We're going down!" as the web was brushed away.

I enjoyed those moments, or following toads or chasing lizards because I thought delight was among the things I had lost; having never exercised the muscle much and having had little reason to try in recent years. The moments didn't last, and I didn't expect them to. But they came back, and that was the pleasant surprise.

. . .

I said there were about eighty two thousand blazes of white paint marking the Appalachian Trail. They were two inches by six inches, and they were splashed on trees and rocks from Georgia to Maine. It was a joke among hikers that it was impossible to get lost. I managed to do it several times.

I never got lost wandering in the woods or taking trailless routes over mountains. It always happened on the trail. Side trails, local trails and spurs were marked with blue and yellow blazes. I was color blind, and faded blue blazes and faded white blazes both look grey to me. I took a few scenic detours because of that. More often, I just didn't pay attention.

One late afternoon, when the sheet metal sky hung heavy with the threat of rain, I turned off the trail to take a break at a shelter. My goal that day, for no particular reason, was to hike thirty miles. The guidebook indicated I'd covered about twenty six miles and a few thousand vertical feet. Several miles back I had come up a mountain pitched so that at times I was using my hands like climbing a ladder. The trailblazers of that section must have been absent the day switchback was taught. Summer was preparing to hand off to fall. At the higher elevations the leaves had begun to turn, and the temperatures dropped. I was tired.

At the shelter I met a mute and a fat guy with plumber's crack. It took a lot of man hours to maintain a couple thousand miles of trail and a few hundred shelters, but this was the first time I had actually seen any volunteers. They were working on the roof. One was a heavy set man who wore suspenders to hold up his tool belt, but they did not hold up his pants. The other couldn't talk. I discovered this when I said hello, and he sort of clucked at me, and the fat guy told me. I'd never met a mute but certainly thought the world could use a few more of them. I wanted to ask what actually caused him to be mute, but that would have been rude and counterproductive. Plumber's crack talked enough for both of them.

"Hallooo, welcome to Eagle's Nest shelter. Don't mind our fix it job. How are ya?"

"Hi." I dropped my pack and dropped myself onto the wood slat floor.

"You look like you been rode hard and put up wet." I didn't know what that meant, but I grunted affirmation. I lay looking up at the menacing clouds and the falling sawdust between us.

"Look! An Eastern Tailed Blue. My god, they're beautiful," Plumber's crack said. I lifted my head to see the flit of deep blue to black wings. It was the butterfly that had made me think I should know more about butterflies. Plumber's crack was really a butterfly guy.

"You know the little yellow ones?" I asked.

"Buttercups."

"What?"

"They're called Buttercups, or Phoebis trite. They're common to the eastern U.S but also found in Asia and South America."

"Buttercups," I said, pleased to meet you. I laid my head back down and listened to him carry on a running conversation with the mute guy and me. There was a mama black bear in the area with two cubs. The forecast called for a severe storm that night, but they were wrong half the time. The roof had held up a good ten years with no repairs. That first sip of beer back home was sure going to taste good. He went on.

I rallied, thanked them for their service, and got on my way. I wanted to do my four miles before the sky blew open. I pressed as hard as my tired legs would go and looked for Buttercups. The wind was whipping, and there were no butterflies to be found. I leaned in and stared down for an hour and a half and called it a day. I got my tent up just as the rain started to spit and fell asleep listening to drums of thunder.

• • •

I awoke, stiff and still tired, to a dark morning and decided there would be no more thirty mile days. The rain was falling in buckets, and the trees were shaking in the wind. Wisps of fog clung thick on the ground. I stuck a water bottle out to catch a torrent coming off the tent and cooked oatmeal under the rain fly. I could see my breath. It was the sort of day that, if you were home, you'd stay on the couch with a comforter and a book and maybe make hot cocoa. I pulled my sleeping bag around me and ate my breakfast.

Fuck ups in back country occurred due to any number of reasons; being ill equipped, ignorance, carelessness, fatigue, panic, or others.

I was already soaked and shivering by the time I broke down my tent and cinched up my pack. With painful, swollen fingers, I fumbled with the buckles. Getting on the move warmed me up a little, and I slogged along. After a few miles I started a long, steep descent. I was happy to be getting off the mountain. The trail dropped straight down the gut and reminded me of the ascent the day before. The run off was pouring down the mountain, and there was as much waterfall as trail. I sidestepped down carefully and explored ahead with the stick. I could not see my feet in the torrent.

In the forest, amid the screech of the wind, I heard limbs snapping and the dull thud of rocks tumbling. That stadium roar of noise was in stark contrast to the utter silence I had so often found. It was disconcerting. I stepped and prodded, stepped and prodded. Above me a bird flapped mightily and moved steadily backward.

It was dumb luck that I paused and looked up the mountain to see a basketball sized rock bounding down the waterfall/trail. I dove to the side, but it caught the sole of my boot. The thick rubber absorbed the force, but I was still spun around and went careening down. Along the slide my thigh raked exposed rock. I maneuvered so I was going feet first and dug them in. I slowed to a stop in a grove of sapling birches.

Triage revealed both my pack and I had nice gashes. During the fall my right wrist was wrenched back; which is anything more than about twenty degrees for the nearly fused bones. It throbbed while I pulled up the leg of my shorts to watch the open wound on my thigh refill with red as fast as the rain washed it away. I duct taped my leg and my pack and decided they could both wait until I was off the mountain.

I leaned on the stick and limped. My hands were white and pruned. I knew the mountain rose about eight hundred vertical feet from its base, and I couldn't be far from the bottom. Getting to the bottom seemed important. Slipping, sliding, wincing, and swearing, I reached horizontal ground. I reached railroad tracks slicing a swath through nowhere.

The problem was I had crossed these tracks yesterday. I stood and stared. I was quivering, but I tried to will my head to operate clearly. Blood was running down my leg and into my boot. I decided there must have been a fork, and I had taken a blue route loop. I turned around and looked up through fog at the mountain I had just fallen down. The rain pelted me, and I limped forward. Getting back to the top seemed important.

The ascent was painful and arduous. It involved crawling, feeling like I was creeping up a garden hose, lots of profanities, and it took hours. When I crested, I lay in the mud and watched my breath. My wrist and thigh were pulsing. My calf was pink in the mixture of blood and rain running down it. The goal stuck in my head having been to get back to the top, I didn't really know what to do then. It did occur to me that it was warmer at the bottom.

I moved mostly because I was cold if I didn't. So, I limped along and reached my camp spot from the night before. I found that funny and laughed in the tempest. I considered turning around at that point and retracing until I found the point where I had deviated in the first place, but I had enough clarity to know I needed shelter.

I pushed on slowly and returned to the Eagle's Nest in the dark; although the cut off for it seemed to be on the wrong side of the trail. Within its shelter, I lit my stove. It took a few shaking matches to get the job done. The heat felt good on my hands, but I was still shivering in my sleeping bag. I knew hypothermia required a more substantial external heat source.

After stumbling around in the dark I remembered I had a headlamp, and I gathered sopping wood. I recognized that forgetting I had a flashlight was a sign of incoherency, and I tried to be methodical as best I could. Toilet paper and the guidebook were all the paper products I had, and they were too damp to light. I whittled twigs down to their dry cores. I shaved sticks until I had dry peelings. My hands shook, and I cut myself a few times. Eventually I had a pile I thought would catch flame. I propped up the pack cover around the precious pile to keep the wind away.

It wasn't until the third heartbreaking match that it caught. I fed it with care as it grew, and I stacked branches around it to dry in the heat. I hobbled into the woods to collect bigger fuel and returned dragging a deadfall tree. The fire was jumping three feet into the air, and I sat back in the heat and brewed tea. When the tree burned through the middle, I pulled both ends into the embers, and the flames shimmied even higher.

Warm and dry, I peeled back my clothing to check the wound. I pulled off the duct tape to look at a rip in my leg. It had stopped bleeding, and the separated flesh looked like sushi. I poured the last of the rubbing alcohol in the gash and wondered why I hadn't used it to start the fire. That fucking hurt, and I yelled within the torrent. I was not quite so much Achilles crying out. I packed the tear with gauze and fashioned strips of duct tape to pull the lips of flesh together. I would add another scar to the collection. The physical scars did not bother me. My fire sizzled and snapped in the rain. By firelight I sewed the rip in my pack. It might have been more exciting if I had to sew my leg, but I didn't.

After two packages of instant pasta-they were fettucine alfredo and spicy pepper-a few cups of tea-it was English breakfast-a slug of Southern Comfort, and a Percocet, I lay next to the fire and watched the rapidly clearing sky. Orion's belt showed between passing clouds like blinking Christmas lights. I pulled out the guidebook, and it showed my original mistake was turning the wrong way on the trail when I had left the Eagle's Nest shelter the day before. Actually, my original fuck up was pushing myself to the point when I made wrong turns and didn't remember I had a guidebook.

The night was sharp. There was the threat of frost. I had a big ass fire and a full belly. I stood, leaning on my stick and wrapping my sleeping bag around me like a Native American with a buffalo hide, and I looked into the darkness. The cicadas were squawking. An owl sounded off in the distance. I might have danced if I could have.

• • •

It was a small, dead end canyon. Cool and dark like a root cellar, the granite pressed in on both sides with harsh angles and sharp edges. A few scattered ferns and mushrooms called it home. I sat at the end staring at the rock wall in front of me. The only exit was back the way I'd come. The

Percocet, Vicodin, and Trazodone bottles were lined up in front of me.

The demons always exhumed. I smelled the stagnant odor of dirt that never dried out. Sometimes there was an impetus, what the psychiatrists called stressors; memories of a dead child, chronic pain, a letter from the I.R.S., that kind of shit. There had been no stressor. There was just an urge to find a dark, quiet place and get things over with.

A spider dangled near me, busy with its knitting.

I wondered what Quinn was doing at that moment. My youngest daughter was almost fifteen. The sun I couldn't see was somewhere high above. She might be hanging with her friends, talking about boys, making videos of them seeing how many marshmallows they could stuff into their mouths. The spider hurried up a line as if it realized it had forgotten something important.

Where was the BSW at that moment? Maybe running a focus group, shuttling kids, or taking a nap. Naps were her favorite. The spider returned to the work site. It was silent in that little slot of rock. My breaths, fast and shallow, echoed back to me in the quiet. I read the warning label on the Trazodone bottle: *"May cause drowsiness."* What bureaucrat decided to warn us about drowsiness on a bottle of fucking sleeping pills?

I opened the Percocet and dumped them onto my bandana. There were one hundred and twenty two of them. It would take at least sixty five. I counted out seventy to be sure. One pill impaired me. It was a big pile. What would seventy do? The spider had moved to the right as if six inches over there might be better hunting. I crushed it between my thumb and index finger and wiped its remains on my shorts.

Candide moved through the best of all possible worlds. He was a fucking idiot. Who was I to judge? I'd tilted at more windmills than Quixote. I took a sip of water and picked up three of the Percocet. It was hard to swallow any more than that. An ant had scurried onto my shorts to investigate the spider guts. I mercifully ended its life too.

I came. I tried. I failed. Put that on my tombstone.

The Percocet were perfect little disks about a quarter inch across with sharp, clean edges. They were serious and efficient pills. I watched a trickle of water that seeped from the stone. Pressure pushed it up and out of the dark, quiet earth, and it ended up in stinking, rotting mud. Pressure did that.

I gathered up the pills and put them back in the bottle. It was another moment of failure, of cowardice. Some mental health professionals speculated that mental illness is like addiction. There was no cure. Vigilance and remission were the best to hope for. Of course, they needed cash flow. The demons laughed in the shadows of my mind, and I picked up my pack.

• • •

That night, I met a communist. His trail name was Tolstoy, and I wanted to point out how stupid that was. The shelter was already crowded with five people when I arrived, but I thought it better to stay than to camp alone. I gave Red Rum some garlic. He gave me a hot sauce packet from a Mexican fast food chain. Ozzy and Harriet, he was from Australia and she was his wife, had resupplied recently and shared a fifth of Jameson's. Another guy snored in a corner.

"I'm a communist," Tolstoy announced. I looked at him. "Well, I'm really more of a socialist." He was probably in his mid twenties with black, heavy framed glasses, a frizzy pony tail, and the requisite beard. I guessed he was a grad student and that his hike was a mommy and daddy funded break from his studies.

"Really?" I said. It wasn't actually a question. Tolstoy looked at me over his glasses.

"Great. We'll share your food then," Ozzy said.

"I'm a social anarchist," Red Rum said, and they all turned to look at him. "Not really. I am a Bears fan though." Ozzy passed him the bottle.

"I like bears," Harriet said.

"Not those bears, honey. It's an American football team."

"You're making fun of me," Tolstoy said.

"Me?" I asked. Tolstoy pushed his glasses back up his nose as if to demonstrate his disdain. I looked at him. I had a strong urge to punch him in the face and explain I didn't give a damn about whatever manufactured trauma he thought he had.

"Just takin' the piss," Ozzy said.

We all sat at the rough wooden table with our little camp stoves. I stirred the hot sauce into my rice and added a package of tuna. Red Rum passed me the Jameson's. Keegan loved Jameson's. I took a sip and estimated its weight in my hand.

"It's bloody heavy, mate. Drink some more."

"What are you, Polar?" Tolstoy asked. He was holding his glasses in his hand and nibbling on an ear piece. I still wanted to punch him. I stirred my pot some more.

"A bitter cynic." In that instance, the truth was a more caustic response.

"Better than a nihilist," Red Rum adjusted the flame on his stove. Harriet was slicing a cucumber.

"Better than a Bear's fan," Ozzy said. Harriet took a drink.

"Harriet knows more about football than you do," Red Rum said. Dinners were completed, and there were the small sounds of vacuums as stoves were shut off. The eating was done in mostly silence. Hikers did not mess around with food. Pots were washed. Food bags on lines were tossed over high branches. Ozzy passed the whiskey around again.

"Why are you a cynic, Polar?" Harriet asked.

"Mind your business, girl," Ozzy said.

"Does he ever wake up?" I gestured toward snoring guy.

"Only when he's hiking, and not always then," Red Rum said.

"The existentialists were called cynics, but they weren't," Tolstoy said.

"Who?" Red Rum asked.

"Did you ever go to school?"

And so it went. Red Rum explained why slasher movies were cautionary tales. Harriet offered me a piece of chocolate that I declined. Tolstoy and Red Rum argued over where they should camp the next night. Tolstoy was apparently finished with me. Ozzy studied a map, and snoring guy continued. I lay back and listened. They were like a family bound by shared experience and a common objective instead of DNA. They would reach the end of the trail, and their family would be no more. Promises would be made to write and call. Contact would diminish over time. People always left. They just didn't know it yet.

I looked out toward the trees in the darkening evening. A few bats fluttered above. At least for that night, being with those people was probably better than the alternative.

• • •

I snaked beneath a forest of oaks and maples and the occasional beech.

Chokecherries, wild blueberries and sumac clogged the ground. In this place the trail was barely wide enough for my boots. I could see just a few feet into the undergrowth.

The cub appeared out of the brush, and he stopped on the strip of trail. His legs seemed slightly too long for his body. His coat appeared to be fluffy, and he was a little on the fat side. He was a real life teddy bear, fifty pounds or so. I froze so as not to scare him, and we appraised each other. My first thought was how incredibly cute he was. My second was wondering where his mother was. He was perhaps twenty feet away.

She came out of the bushes just behind him. A strand of blueberry stem hung from her mouth. She nuzzled the air with her nose then turned toward me. According to the guides, female black bears are around two hundred fifty pounds. I compared her to guys I knew who clocked in at that weight. She seemed much bigger.

She snorted and pawed at the ground, but then found a shrub that was more interesting than I. The cub whined and rubbed against her leg like a cat might do. She was a little bow legged, and the hump of her back was the height of my chest. She looked at me occasionally, down the blonde hair of her muzzle, with black eyes that were disproportionately small for her head. She raked the dirt with claws the length of my fingers, and I wondered what she might be trying to dig up. A stray beam of sunlight slanted across her face. The cub had more interest in me, surveying just as much as I was.

I stayed still and watched them. It was always a deliciously jarring experience to be confronted with my true position on the food chain. A single unarmed man was not king of the jungle….or the forest. I wasn't in any real danger as long as I didn't do anything stupid like try to pet the cub. Black bears were notoriously chicken, even running away from poodles, and she was busy consuming calories for the coming winter. So I watched the magnificent creature and her child.

I had snorkeled above a school of sharks once and watched a grizzly from a quarter mile downwind in Yellowstone. I lay in tall grass and cringed every time he looked my way. A wolf tracked me on a hike in the Sawtooths, trailing a hundred yards off to my left and stopping stone still whenever I looked his way. He got bored after a while, or maybe stopped letting me see him. I had heard a mountain lion scream on a black night in a high mountain camp and once had a pack of coyotes surround my tent in a southern desert. They yipped and sniffed and eventually went away. I don't know what actual peril I was ever in at those times, but I *felt* as if I had just stared across the dusky threshold of death, and perception begets the reality. And I felt alive, really alive.

I reached for the pocket on my pack belt where my camera was, and both bears looked at me. By the time I had it out, she had turned into the forest, and I got a picture of a swaying bear ass with a small paw swatting at it.

When I went through airborne school in the army, there were about four hundred students in my class. An instructor told us roughly one out of every five hundred parachutes fail. With five jumps for each of us, that meant there would be about four screamers, as they called the failed chutes. At the altitude we were jumping from, in the event of a screamer you had about six seconds to release the main chute and pull the emergency one before you augured into the ground at terminal velocity. Standing in the open door of an airplane in flight was a nut crunching experience in itself. The added consideration that the chute on your back might be the unlucky screamer was cause enough for many to step away from the door and be booted from the program. But if you stepped out the door, into the void, it was pure euphoria when the chute caught the air, and you were drifting like a dandelion seed.

My suicidal moments ironically produced a similar experience. They lasted a day or a week, but I invariably felt much better after failing to kill myself. It was not a good prescription, but it produced excellent results. Perhaps it was affirmation of our mortality that jolted our appreciation for the time preceding the end. In the aftermath of our fight or flight moments, the leftover adrenaline was like crack for the soul.

• • •

It was an unseasonably warm November day. Indian summer lingered. I was outside tossing a ball for Bailey. With each throw he bounded down the hill, heaved himself into the sea and sloshed proudly back with his prize.

My home was a six hundred square foot bungalow. It was close to a hundred years old, and "fixer upper" did not begin to describe it. The roof sagged. Anything round on the floor would roll, and the floorboards creaked with any application of weight. The house behind was so close I could hear my neighbor snore. But out my back door I looked at open water. I figured they weren't making any more coastline and someday I'd build a new house.

Each morning brought an array of sea birds. A family of twenty one swans paraded by every day. One was an ugly grey and stood out amid his stark white friends. The BSW always counted them to make sure all were well. Low tides brought hundreds of seagulls. Geese rested in the bay on their way to wherever geese go. Ducks quickly figured out they were safe from hunters there because I would release Bailey to bound down and send them into scattered flight much to the chagrin of the camouflaged douche bags in the bushes. Cormorants would sun themselves and spread their wings to dry on Scylla and Charybdis; the rocks out in the bay that I named. Gangly terns walked like clowns on stilts in the marsh.

I was happy in my shack by the sea. The phone rang. I ignored it and tossed the ball again for Bailey. When I went back inside, I checked the message.

"Finn, you need to call home. Keegan has been killed." That was the voicemail. I saved it for over a year and would listen to it when I had any doubts the world was full of insensitive pricks. It wasn't "Please call home. There's been a tragedy." He couldn't even temper it by saying Keegan had passed away or even just died. No, I learned my son was gone in a concise, heartless, seven second message.

I called his mother and learned my son was the victim of a hit and run. The police were investigating.

There were no life experiences, no self help manual, no education, nothing to prepare one for such news. I truly didn't know what to do. I knew the news would travel fast. I knew the phone would start ringing. I didn't know what to say to anyone calling. So, I walked down to the beach.

The water had long begun to turn cold, but I waded in the waves. I walked back and forth. I stared out at the water and back at the land. I started to cry, stopped, started and stopped a few more times, and continued to wade. The news was really more than my brain could fathom. Even in hindsight, I don't think we're adequately wired to process such news. My son was dead. So, I waded. It seemed as good a response as any at the time. I scraped my feet across mussel beds and my ankles through sea grass already retreating from the coming cold. The smell of low tide was all around.

I picked up shells and skipped rocks. I waded until my feet and ankles were numb. It was an adult version of covering my ears and going "la la la la". I could not cope. I did not want my mind to go to memories. They would be unbearable. So, I sat in the cold, damp sand and wove a little rope out of sea grass.

The sun was melting deep behind me and fog was entering the bay. The BSW came. My little rope was a couple feet long. She put a coat over my shoulders and sat in the sand next to me. She put her hand on mine, and I sobbed. I cried until stars appeared above. Orion's belt was low on the horizon in front of me, and I cried out at the sight of it.

Part 2

Events occur and sometimes nothing is ever the same again. The big bang and the Fosbury flop were certainly game changers. I was arthritic, unemployed, clinically depressed, occasionally suicidal, disconnected from my living son, unable to let go of the dead one, and broke. It would have been easy to lay the events out chronologically and blame each on its predecessor, but that wouldn't tell the whole story. Lives and history were full of nuance and shades of detail. A timeline did not reflect an individual's role in the weaving of their own tapestry. It did not reveal the awesome power of compounding. Odysseus had a lot of shit happen to him and gutted it out. Kurtz snapped under the pressure. Candide just grinned like an imbecile. I went for a long walk.

I had been told I had good reasons to be depressed. That didn't really help. Validation never interested me. Others told me I need to just suck it up and drive on. The implication being I could overcome the dump truck of shit that tipped on me, and I just didn't. I resisted my urge to say "fuck you," to those people because there was probably a time when I could have. I mentioned compounding. The events don't just add like blocks in a wall. They multiply intensity like a pyramid. Each successive block adds weight to all those beneath it. Still, through all of it, I played a role. I was not an innocent victim in my own story.

Early in my hike the BSW called to tell me the storage unit I had rented was getting ready to auction the remaining possessions I had in the world. She had paid the bill, and I just needed to log on and ensure the payment was received. I could not do it. The possibility of any more bad news was beyond my scope. The turtle is safer inside his shell.

My new and bigger shell was the Appalachian Trail. I walked. I found water. Those were the extent of my obligations. I regulated my exposure to others as I saw fit. Nature, being immune to our plights, tossed me the occasional challenge. By and large, they were problems I was equipped to deal with.

Polar was not facing exponential growth.

I was pondering these things when I first met Merlin. I came up behind him. His grey ponytail bounced as he labored up a hill. I settled in behind him on the trail and waited for a wide spot to get by.

"Are you going to fucking pass me?" He hollered without looking back, breaking his pace or moving over. His pack was worn and had several patches of duct tape.

"Waiting for a wide spot."

"I don't like tailgaters."

"Sorry."

"Don't apologize. Just move on." He stopped and moved one foot off the trail. I walked past. He had a long grey beard and wore round, wire rimmed glasses.

"Thanks. Have a good hike."

"What the hell's that supposed to mean?"

That afternoon I came upon a beautiful spot amid giant boulders and overlooking a valley. Orderly fields were far below. I pitched my tent and made some tea. I was sitting, shirtless and barefoot, writing in the leather bound journal when Merlin came trudging in.

"Nice spot." He dropped his pack and pulled off his boots.

"Seriously?"

"Do you own this spot?"

"No."

"Then I guess we're sharing."

He quickly used sticks, rope and a tarp to rig a shelter. I put on my headphones and watched the hawks in the valley below. After a few songs I was hit with a pebble. I pulled out the headphones and looked at him.

"I'm talking to you," he said.

"You hit me with a rock?"

"Want some soup?" It smelled good. I wanted to tell him to fuck off.

"What's in it?"

"Picky? Wild onions, herbs and bouillon."

It was delicious. Except for blueberries and some shitty dandelion tea, I had not attempted to forage.

"Are those mushrooms?" I asked and poked in my pot.

"I knew you wouldn't eat it if I said there was."

He was eating it too so I figured we could enjoy acute abdominal pain together if he was wrong. I thanked him for the soup and climbed back up on a rock. I fingered my sea grass rope. It was beginning to fray.

I was awake and sitting on a rock when he arose around four a.m. I offered coffee and gestured toward my cooking pot. He filled his cup and stared at me. I hated when people, even the BSW, stared at me.

"What?"

He said nothing but shuffled barefoot off into the dark forest. He returned holding the hem of his shirt up to carry blackberries. We ate the berries in silence by sinking moonlight. I looked at him sidelong. He was gaunt even by hiker standards, and I wondered if he ate anything except what he found. He was packed up before dawn had any traction in the sky.

"Have a good hike," he said. I pictured him smirking in the darkness. He walked away.

"Asshole," I said quietly.

"Dickhead," he called back from the dark.

I caught him again around midmorning and offered a good morning as I passed. He commented on the beauty of the day. I continued on.

In the afternoon I saw a whitetail doe and her fawn nibbling in a glade. Their ears perked up, and they paused to look at me. I did not advance. The fawn returned to eating. He was starting to get his winter coat, and the speckles on his back were fading. The doe's features were delicate as if carefully sculpted. I watched them for some time until a group of Girl Scouts came swarming down the trail. The deer bolted at the shrieks.

I politely answered their questions about how far I'd hiked, how long I'd been out, what my trail name was, if I got scared, and had I seen any bears. This was a regular event on the trail. Youth group leaders view section and through hikers as interactive zoo exhibits. I tolerated this because at least the kids were out in the woods, and there was a good chance the Girl Scouts might give cookies.

The wilderness tract flanking the trail narrowed then, and "no camping" signs were posted. I would have to stay at a shelter that night. It was a three walled cinder block structure with bunks. There was a well with a bright yellow pump, a brick fire pit and a swath of mown grass. I put up my tent on the lawn.

Merlin came in a couple hours later.

"You again. Did you pass those girls?" He asked.

"Yeah."

"God damn kids."

I imagined their encounter with Merlin was slightly traumatic. He dumped an assortment of plants on the ground, got a small fire going and put a pot of water on it to boil. He sat on the ground with his legs crossed and sliced his plants.

"Wild carrots, poor man's pepper, and some burdocks," he said.

"Pasta primavera and tuna." I stirred my own pot.

"Put some of this in it," and he tossed some sliced stems to me. They definitely added flavor to my meal.

I lay back to wait for stars. Merlin stripped naked and gave himself a bath at the yellow pump.

• • •

Fourteen hours after I learned of Keegan' death I was on a plane heading back to Denver. The BSW had organized the flight, hotel and rental car while I sat on the couch staring at the bookshelf and considering various ways to organize the books. I ordered a bloody mary and asked for two mini bottles of vodka. I had not eaten or slept, and the alcohol burned my stomach. The BSW would be a couple days behind me because she had to take care of some work. I wished she was with me.

Trips home were painful under the best of circumstances. The house I had bought, the home we had made, was no longer mine. All evidence that I had ever been there was eradicated long ago. The kitchen my dad, Keegan and I had remodeled was not mine. I was not allowed upstairs to the bedroom. I had to ring the doorbell.

My ex, Sarah, answered the door, and we hugged. I could see my former in-laws had come in force. They were an odd but fiercely loyal family. They spent most of their time arguing and fighting with one another but always rallied to their own in a crisis. I had no expectations that any of my family would show. I met her boyfriend. He seemed like a decent guy. Quinn came into the room. Her face was puffy and tear-streaked. I held her tight. She adored her big brother.

I sat on the couch and held Quinn. Sarah's brother did shots of tequila and told jokes to fill in the silence. Her father stared at a beer. Her mother cooked and let out an occasional wail. Her sister glared at me. It reminded me that I had paid her college tuition one semester, and she never paid me back. People began to arrive bearing casseroles, stews and lasagnas. They used to be our friends. She got most of those in the divorce too.

Terri from up the street arrived. Never a thin woman, she was packing some weight. It seemed she had not bought any new clothes to accommodate the added pounds. Her shirt looked like it might rip at the seams. I said hello. She gave me a disdainful look and called Quinn to come sit with her. I sat alone at the end of the couch and wondered which level of hell this might be. Sarah and I talked briefly about meeting the next day to begin the arrangements, and I said I was going to my hotel.

"This is your home. This is your family. You shouldn't be alone." It was a nice gesture even if not true. I was driving past the high school, a few blocks from the house, when Quinn called and asked if she could come with me. It would be a lie to say that didn't bring a small smile.

We ordered ice cream from room service and watched a comedy movie on pay per view. Occasionally she would begin to cry, and I would hold her. Occasionally, I cried, and she held me. We told funny Keegan stories like the time he tried to sneak out of the house at night and broke his arm or when he high centered his car on a snow bank. When she was around three years old, she used to take his food and say, "We share, 'kay?" I don't know if it was a good way to address the tragedy, but it seemed right.

It took a week to complete the process of the cremation and the service. It was held at Sarah's new age church and involved a gong. The BSW arrived after a couple days. We showed up at the house one morning and Sarah asked us to come back later. Guess it wasn't my home after all. I broke down in the service and could not read the words I had written.

My sister did not come. She probably had a spa day scheduled. My mom said she would plant a tree in the forest for Keegan but could not make it. I didn't bother to call my dad. My friend Mike did show. We had known each other since high school and a shared interest in Dungeons and Dragons. I was best man at his wedding, and he at mine. He and his wife Rene flew out from California as soon as they heard, and they babysat me after the BSW had to leave because she had nobody to watch her kids. He read my words at the service while I sobbed.

I boarded a plane and drank scotch until it landed.

• • •

Merlin again departed in the dim of early morning. I caught up to him in a corn field. It was a challenge to hinge together two thousand miles of wilderness trail through the populace of America's eastern seaboard. In places we wound through farmland to connect the dots. Merlin was loading ears of corn into his pack.

"Doin' a little grocery shopping," he said as I passed. The afternoon carried me through fields of peas, lettuce and a cow pasture until I ascended back into the forest.

I was watching ants transport grains of rice when he approached. By arranging the rice just so, I had them marching in a figure eight. He set about putting up his shelter across the clearing from where my tent was. I sighed.

"It's a big forest," I said. He ignored me. He built a fire and unloaded corn, a plastic bag of peas and a head of lettuce from his pack.

"No beef?"

"Too heavy." He grinned at me. He shaved the corn and shelled the peas into his pot. He tossed the cob into the forest, and a grey squirrel immediately went to investigate. While his food cooked he pulled a plastic bag from his pack that appeared to contain cow shit. He opened it up. It did. He cut mushrooms from it.

"Good stuff," he said.

After his dinner he sat cross legged in the dirt and pulled off his shirt. There was a faded blue tattoo on the papery skin of his shoulder. It was a heart with the name Maria below it. I thought of the tattoo on my back; the Chinese symbol for love and the name Sarah above it. That was a drunken mistake. I went back to reading my book.

"You don't much like people," he said.

I looked up.

"Some."

"Me neither, at least not most."

I thought of saying I didn't much like him. He pulled a bag of cashews from his pack, took a fist full and tossed it to me. I should have just tossed it back. Sharing food on the trail meant connecting. I took a handful and said thank you.

"Where you headed?" he asked.

"Not really sure." I don't know why I gave him the true answer. He laughed. It was a hearty, honest laugh, and it seemed as if even his bones shook.

"Well, you're in the right place then," and he farted. He made no effort to hide it. He even lifted a butt cheek to help it escape. And he laughed again. It occurred to me that if I could learn to tolerate this guy, I could probably cope with just about anyone.

We repeated the pattern for a few more days. I got up some time in the middle of the night. Merlin rose before dawn, had a cup of my coffee and left. I caught him in late morning. He wandered into my camp in the evening bearing whatever flora he'd rummaged that day. We didn't say much except to comment on the weather or the plants he had found.

On the fourth day I found him waiting for me where the trail crossed a highway. There was a small town a couple miles down the road.

"Headin' to resupply. Wanna come?" he asked. I thought about it.

"Okay." I don't know why I agreed. It was a chance to escape him. Still, there was some penance, maybe some exercise of the tolerance muscles, in being with him.

We walked single file on the shoulder. Merlin had a profanity or obscene gesture for just about every car that came by.

"You're bugging me back there. You take the lead." I moved ahead. I could see his shadow and slowed whenever it fell back. A Volvo tore past us. They never moved over.

"Fuckin' asshole," Merlin yelled at the car. "What's the grass rope for?"

"Decoration."

"It's woven like shit."

I saw the shadow of his hand lifting to grab it. I stopped and turned around.

"Don't touch it." We locked eyes for a moment. Another car passed us, and dust swirled about.

"I was just going to tighten up the weave for you." We resumed walking.

"Sorry. It's," I took a few steps on the gravel shoulder of the road, "special."

"I know. People don't hang stupid shit on their packs. Well, they do, but you know what I mean. We need to work on your people skills."

I smiled and kept walking.

It wasn't so much a town as a small collection of stores on the side of a highway. There was a supermarket, a video store, an ice cream shop, a farmer's supply, a bar, and an outfitter. We stopped there.

"I have to take a shit," he said and wandered around the corner of the building.

The outfitter was in a converted house, and there were a picnic table and Adirondack chairs made from skis in the yard. The house was yellow with green and purple shutters. Bent hiking poles stuck in the grass lined the sidewalk up to the covered porch. Kayaks were stacked up on the side. I exchanged pleasantries with the old guy inside, signed his guestbook, and answered that I was hiking to Virginia. I bought some heavy duty thread to fix a rip in my gaiter and a fuel can for my stove and gave him my old one. It wasn't empty yet, but it weighed a few ounces. The cowbell on the door jangled, and Merlin entered.

"The legend!" the shopkeeper said. They hugged. "I heard you were headed this way. I'll grab a couple beers."

"Don't forget Polar."

"Of course. He didn't say he was with you."

"He's shy that way," Merlin said and smirked at me.

We sat in the Adirondack chairs and drank PBR's. The shopkeeper, his name was Three Miles, and Merlin bullshitted and caught up. I learned some things about my new companion. They had met while both were through hiking almost twenty years ago. That was Merlin's second through hike. When he reached Katahdin on that trip he turned around and walked all the way back to Springer Mountain, Georgia. We had a couple more beers. Three Miles told Merlin he could use some help in the shop if he needed a place to winter over.

A woman pulled up in a rusty pickup loaded with kayaks. She and Merlin hugged. Her graying hair was pulled into a braid. One of her Birkenstocks was missing a strap. I held out my hand when we were introduced, and she hugged me too. They called her Frog. Three Miles said they used to call her Pollywog until she got old.

"I have a pot of chili on. Looks like I'll have to make a beer run. Polar, did they show you where everything is?"

"No, ma'am."

"Ma'am? How the hell old do you think I am? C'mon, honey." They lived upstairs above the shop. She gave me a tour, showed me where the towels, bathroom and washing machine were, and told me to help myself to anything I could find. She left to go buy beer. I thought about a shower but felt awkward being alone in their home. I paused to look at an old photo of them. Three Miles had carefully combed hair and wore a suit, and Frog wore pearl earrings. They stood in front of the Empire State Building. There were been many pictures of me in suits somewhere. I carried three beers back outside.

"Got him trained up already," Three Miles said and laughed.

Soon an old Subaru with a Yakima rack and a Jeep pulled up and several people entered the yard. Some wore bandanas on their heads. There was a woman with hairy legs. One man carried a cooler covered with stickers from ski resorts.

"Merlin, you son of a bitch!" One guy said. A lot more hugging and back slapping occurred. I was introduced and shook hands all around. Beers were popped. Laughter drowned out the sound of the stereo in the Jeep. Frog returned with another case of beer. It felt like being at a stranger's family reunion.

I wandered over and sat under the crab apple tree that grew in the corner of the yard and listened to their stories. There was the time Merlin carried Jasmine off a mountain when she broke her leg, when he hiked three hundred miles in nine days to make a friend's funeral, and such. Frog came over with a bowl of chili for me.

"You're alone enough when you're on the trail. Join the party," she said.

"I don't want to intrude." She laughed at me.

"Honey, you come hiking in with Merlin, you're part of the tribe." Then I laughed at both the word and the willing acceptance.

"It's okay to have a little fun," she said and grabbed my wrist to pull me. I winced, and she apologized. She ran her fingers over the bones of my wrist. "Rheumatoid?" she asked, and I nodded.

"Well, that sucks," she said. There was no pity; just acknowledgement and I was appreciative. I rose and joined the raucous circle. A guy called Gizmo handed me a bottle of beer. I told the story of getting lost and falling down the mountain, and they all laughed. The woman with hairy legs, she was called Lobster, said she once hiked a whole state in the wrong direction.

We spent a couple days with Three Miles and Frog. I accepted their offer for the spare bedroom instead of pitching my tent in the back yard. I helped load the kayaks they rented to tourists down at the river. Merlin spent most of the time drinking coffee in the shop and telling customers what not to buy. Members of the tribe came and went.

Frog and I sat on the porch. She was patching a kayak. I was sewing my gaiter. There was a good, strong wind driving the smell of cut grass. Merlin and Three Miles had walked down to the pub to play darts. I pulled out my Skoal and got a dip. Frog asked for the can, and I passed it to her. She put a little dip in her cheek.

"I like a nice chew every now and then," she said. We sat there working and spitting. A pair of blue jays chased the sparrows out of the feeder in the yard.

"You should give yourself a break," she said.

"Huh?" I focused on the stitches.

"You're too hard on yourself. You're not a bad person; at least not any worse than most. Give yourself a break."

"You got all that in two days?"

"I have a Ph.D. in psychology, and I live with hikers. They're the most fucked up people on earth. I know fucked up."

"You're a hiker."

"Exactly."

She told me stories of the tribe. Gizmo caught his wife in bed with another man and almost beat both of them to death. He got out of prison six years ago, hiked the trail, and did volunteer work at the women's shelter. Lobster was a recovering meth addict; clean four years. Her parents had custody of her children and wouldn't allow her to see them. Three Miles was screwed by his business partner, lost everything, and went for a hike. She followed him from the Upper East Side of Manhattan to this place. Merlin first hiked the trail after his wife and son were killed in a car crash. He never really stopped.

"You're not special."

I told her my story, from beginning to present, wholly and without embellishment. The BSW was the only other person who knew it all. I was surprised even as I talked.

"That'll be two hundred dollars," she said. I smiled.

"Fuck you."

"You wish. You're still not special. You just need to heal."

"It's the land of the misfit toys tribe."

"It's just like any other tribe, and you fit right in, honey." She asked to see pictures of my children, and I showed her. Later she commandeered my phone and talked to the BSW. I found that a little odd, but maybe that's what people did. Afterward she told me that I had found a keeper.

"Don't screw it up," she said.

It was morning with a promise of a sunny day. I had loaded the kayaks into the truck. Merlin had drunk coffee. We never did make it to the supermarket, but Three Miles had loaded us up with freeze dried meals. He would not take the money I offered. Merlin had a batch of Frog's special brownies. We were standing in the yard with our packs on. I had a list of phone numbers, email addresses and places to stop along the trail to find more of the tribe. Frog had already friended the BSW on Facebook. I shook hands with Three Miles and Gizmo. Frog and I hugged.

"Don't get lost," she said.

We set off with me in the lead. I glanced back to maintain a pace Merlin could manage. The sun began to burn through the morning fog. He was quiet; not even swearing at the passing cars. We reached the turn off to the trail. It occurred to me that, while every step I took was into new territory, Merlin had traveled that ground four times that I knew of.

"Resupply?" I asked.

"Of the spirit."

"Why'd you invite me?"

"You looked like you could use a good time."

We hiked quietly for a while. I could hear his breath as we ascended up out of the valley. At the crest we turned to look down. The yellow house was far below us in the distance.

"I saw you watching a butterfly," he said. I started to laugh. "Hike your own fucking hike," and he sat down on a log.

"I feel like going slow today," and I sat down.

"Asshole."

"Dickhead." We watched the clouds wander for a while.

"Thank you," I said.

Merlin didn't hike particularly slowly. He just stopped a lot. At some indicator I couldn't fathom, he would wander off the trail. I followed. We found mushrooms. He showed me that the spears of dandelion leaves grow down. Its poisonous cousin's spears point up. We watched a praying mantis stab and eat a spider, and Merlin called that a "fuckin' metaphor."

We made camp in a grove of hemlocks. I showed him that boiling was not the only cooking method. He told me it tasted like shit, and he had a second helping. Despite my best efforts, I had a companion and a tribe. I wasn't sure how I felt about that, but being only unsure was even a little surprising.

"Do you believe in God?" he asked. The fire was dying away, and there was deep dusk above us. I was trying to get a chipmunk to take a crumb from my hand.

"Yes."

"Amazing son of a bitch, God is."

The chipmunk scurried into my palm, grabbed the morsel, and dashed to the rocks.

"Sure."

"I mean look around us. I sometimes forget how amazing it all is."

"You give God a lot of credit."

"He made this," and he held up an acorn. I held up my wrist and turned it; deformed bones on one side, thin scars on the other.

"He made this too."

"You blame him for a lot."

"Take the credit, get the blame."

We sat silently for a while; each of us watching the wilting embers of the fire. The chipmunk came back looking for more. An owl shouted.

"I'm sorry about your son," he said. I looked at him in the gloom. "Tell Frog somethin', it ain't a secret."

I crawled into my tent.

My foot was inflamed the next morning. After a few tries, I gritted my teeth, jerked my boot on, and lay gasping. I didn't catch Merlin that day until I hobbled into his camp at sunset. He silently took my water bladder and left for the spring. I nodded my thanks when he returned.

He set about slicing roots into a pot and boiling it. After a while, he handed me a cup of it.

"Some secret forest remedy?" I asked.

"Soup."

The flare up peaked in the night, and I awoke from my own cry of pain. I popped some narcotics and crawled out of the tent to elevate my feet on a log. I lay there sweating and trying to find the position where my feet hurt the least.

"Can I get you anything?" Merlin asked from the dark.

"No," I said and took a few deep breaths. "Thanks."

The next morning I convinced Merlin there was no benefit in him staying with me. He filled my water bladders and brought me a pile of mushrooms. We made plans, if I didn't catch him in the next few days, to meet in Harper's Ferry. He hiked away, and I was alone in the forest for the first time in a while. It seemed a little odd, but I blamed that on the Percocet.

I sprawled on the ground and stared up through leaves. Most were green, but some were yellow. A Buttercup flitted into my field of view. It tossed about in the breeze and then was carried away as if it meant to go that direction all along. A line of ants marched over my foot and continued away on their mission. I sipped water and soon enough the sun was gone.

The moon rose; just a small slice. Still, I lay there. Crickets began their tune. A possum came to investigate, and it hissed when I lifted my head to look. I had seen the sun rise and set on this piece of forest from my skyward vantage, and I wanted to see it through. I watched time being acutely marked, but there seemed to be no passage of it. I peered up through the dark. Perhaps there was something to learn from this view; given enough time.

I fell asleep at some point after the moon had drifted up and over me. I awoke shivering with the dawn. The pain in my feet had subsided. I seared mushrooms for breakfast and tried to glean something from the sky I had watched. There was no obvious lesson, but gazing always left me feeling there was some incremental change. I just had to figure out what it was. What had Keegan seen when he gazed? I realized it had been two days since I'd spoken to the BSW. I texted her that I was okay. I pulled on my boots, packed up, and I hiked.

. . .

It was a beautiful glade. The melting sun dappled through the leaves making everything speckled. A stream gurgled through the middle. Ferns burst across the forest floor in a cacophony of greens even I could see. I could have gone another eight or so miles before the light failed, but it was too perfect of a spot to pass up.

I found a place where others had camped before. The bare spot was deep and soft with pine needles from the conifers that grew among the deciduous trees. Bare feet propped on the pack, I lay back, listened to the scurrying of small animals, the chatter of the water, and I watched the play of light through the forest. It was cool in that deep spot of the woods, and I thought it would be a good night for a fire. Eventually, I got up to collect wood. There were many tree limbs near the little stream, and I knew it could rage when it felt like it.

The fire snapped. Its refractive light limited my visibility to a few foot radius around me. The pot of water next to it was approaching a boil. I could hear it rolling like miniature thunder. I looked into the darkness with unease. It was the same dark I looked at every night. Perhaps it was the limits the fire created on my vision. A twig snapped somewhere out in the dark. I flicked on my headlamp but saw nothing.

After dinner I fed the fire and pulled out my phone. In the directory were numbers for Keegan, Quinn, Duncan and Shane. Shane was my oldest daughter. Quinn was the baby. After Quinn's birth Shane demanded that Quinn be given a boy's name also. I could have called Quinn or Shane. I dialed Keegan and listened to his voicemail message. It was still good to hear his voice.

I knew it was a mistake, but I pulled out the pictures. There was the one of all four of them on a bridge in Virginia. Keegan was sixteen with the traces of a beard he was trying to grow. Quinn was fourteen and just sprouting into the beauty that would later have me chasing boys off my porch. Duncan was six and already too much like me. Shane was four and clinging to her favorite stuffed animal, a Labrador named Black Licorice. There was the picture of Keegan holding Shane before his prom. There was Shane singing in her middle school play. She was the good witch in *Wicked*. There was the picture of Duncan at his graduation that I pulled off Facebook.

The fire was dying, and the darkness closed in. I tossed a few branches on to push it back. I pulled out my knife and carved on my stick for a while. Then, I shaved some of its tip into the fire. It was a good knife, and I kept it sharp. I held it to my arm and slid it, with the sharp edge away, down; back and forth as if whetting it. Still, hair came off and small drops of blood appeared where the serrated section of the blade caught skin.

I held it at my wrist; parallel to my arm. I had learned in the nut house that cutting across is much more difficult. I held it there. The tip dug into my skin but did not break the surface. I made a fist and could see the veins emerge. I traced them with just the tip of the knife. It was like coloring with an invisible crayon. Just a little more pressure, and I could color with vivid red.

It was a picture of Quinn that caused me to pause. We were skiing at Mary Jane. It was a warm spring day, and she had unzipped the layers of coats I had embedded her in. She was eager to try out her first blue run, and she went careening down it, jacket flying in the wind, until she ended up in a yard sale crash with half her equipment left behind. I raced to catch up and found her sitting in the snow laughing deep from her belly. I snapped a picture.

I put away the knife and pissed on the fire to extinguish it. My eyes adjusted in the dark, but I could still not see any stars through the forest above. An owl called above me. Another one answered. They carried on a conversation. I listened and clung to each whooo and call and screech from the darkness because they pulled me away from a darker purpose.

. . .

Two days later I found Merlin in the frozen food aisle in a podunk Maryland town. Some towns embrace hikers. Some eschew them. You can tell as soon as you walk in. I had hiked in for some ice cream. I guess Merlin had done the same. I was behind him. He was in his normal attire of too short shorts and holey t-shirt.

A couple, I guessed husband and wife, approached from the other direction. The man leaned in and hit Merlin's basket. His fruit and ice cream went rolling. He looked at the floor and stooped to gather up his groceries. A nasty smile spread across the man's face.

"Freak," he said and looked back at Merlin as they passed. Merlin was on his hands and knees and did not look up.

I knew this man; or at least his type. He was wearing a Ravens jersey and an adjustable baseball cap on backwards. The plastic strap was cutting into his forehead. He had a beer gut and basketball shoes that probably cost more than he'd spent on the woman in the past year.

"Fucking asshole," I said as they passed by me, and I kept walking. He outweighed me by at least sixty pounds, and I knew he'd do the mental math.

"What did you fucking say?" he said. I stopped and turned around. I set my basket on the floor.

"Which word didn't you understand?"

The woman held onto his hand, and he shrugged her off to approach me. He was going for a chest bump, but his gut hit me first. I was pushed back by his weight. He pressed me against the frozen pizza case. He was breathing heavily, and he smelled like Old Spice. I held his stare and breathed slowly in through my nose. Merlin and the woman watched us.

"I'll fucking kill you," he said, and he slapped me. Guys who don't know how to fight always lead with their chest and follow with a slap.

My elbow hit his eye socket just before my knee hit his groin. He was already falling, but I punched him two more times as he went down; once to the mouth and once to the nose. Blood sprayed. I regretted the punches as soon as they landed as pain shot through my hands. Despite the pain, it felt so good to hit that guy. He lumped into the fetal position. I pushed him onto his back with the heel of my boot and spit on his face.

"Freak," I said. I picked up my basket and got two bags of frozen strawberries for my hands. Merlin was still staring at the man on the ground. I picked up his basket too and went to the checkout.

Outside we packed up the groceries. I walked with the cold strawberries in my hands, and we disappeared into the forest.

"That was messed up," Merlin said behind me.

"Yeah."

"I mean you beating him up."

"He swung first." I passed over a long brown centipede being eaten by ants.

"You provoked him."

We walked in silence for a while. There was only the sound of breathing and boots scraping rocks.

"I don't like bullies," I said. My hands were throbbing, and the melting strawberries were leaking red juice as I walked.

We stopped to eat the berries under a spreading pine. Red sticky juice ran down our arms and faces. Merlin looked like a vampire that had just fed. I probably looked the same. Bees hummed about.

"Remind me not to piss you off," Merlin said. I held up my swollen hands. The fingers looked like overstuffed sausages.

"I can't get pissed off too often."

That night I fried peaches with wild onions and some chili powder to go with a couple packs of tuna. Merlin found mushrooms, and I made something vaguely like a risotto. He did a little jig while I cooked. I stuck my hands in a pot of cold spring water periodically.

"Feels good, huh?" I asked.

"What?"

"Some getting their due."

"Yeah," and he stopped his dance, "but it shouldn't."

"No, but it does."

. . .

The starfish plunked into the water. She picked up another and tossed it back to the sea. A strong storm the night before had washed hundreds of them onto the shore. The BSW had set to rescuing them. We wandered along saving starfish. The sky was still grey with leftover storm. She chased away the seagulls that came for the buffet.

I wrapped my pinkie finger around her index finger. It was how we held hands when my arthritis was acting up. The sand on that stretch of beach was not fine granules. It was thick and chunky. I stepped gingerly with still winterized bare feet. She stooped for another starfish. It was blue and had six tentacles. She talked to it in the voice she reserved for plants and animals she deemed most in need of a kind word. Plunk it went into the sea.

I watched as she picked up a slipper shell to admire. Then she found a razor clam jutting up and yelled in delight about how rare they were. It oozed a long sticky tongue around her hand, and she dropped it with a shriek. I laughed. Still, she picked it up and put it back in the water.

It was a Sunday morning in the April before Keegan died. Most Sundays found us wandering the beach after coffee and the paper. She always found delight in a pebble or a shell or a horseshoe crab. I watched her wade in the waves. Without makeup, still with bedhead, her jeans rolled up to her knees and wearing my old hooded sweatshirt, I found her to be her most beautiful.

"What?" she asked.

"You're very beautiful."

"Are you on Percocet?" she asked, and she smiled.

"Not at the moment." It was our common refrain.

Seven months later we sat in a bar in Denver after another day of funeral planning. Sarah's pastor had been careful to say the meeting was for family only. The BSW put her hand on my arm as I prepared to start a fight, and I stayed silent. She went outside and fed geese. I sat and listened to Sarah's mom wail and a debate about the appropriate number of times to ring a gong and what color balloon release would be most meaningful. I understood that memorials were for the living, not the dead, but...fuck.

I ordered a Fat Tire and a shot of Jameson's. I didn't like whiskey, but Jameson's was Keegan' favorite. We had many long debates and discussions in that bar about the Avalanche's chances in the playoffs, the best of the Lord of the Rings movies, the possibility of interstellar travel, the meaning of life, and such.

I set that bar on fire once. The company I worked for was closing the Denver regional office. I would work from home, but the seven other people in the office were losing their jobs. I wasn't supposed to tell them until the last Friday when the office was shut down, but I did. Each of them showed up and worked hard until the end. I would take them to that bar for unhappy hour. We were there on that last day. Someone ordered a round of Flaming Dr Peppers. I didn't know what they were, but they were on fire. I accidentally knocked mine over, and the varnish on the bar burst into flames. The bartender's nicely tossed bucket of mop water prevented a disaster. The bartender remembered me.

She rubbed my neck; aware of the ghosts flanking me. She had her nails done, and it reminded me of the first night I met her. I looked at the bar. It had been refinished since the fire. I had been dealing with the abstract concept that my son was gone. Being there was concrete. Keegan and I would not again order big prime ribs with baked potatoes. He wouldn't humor me any more by listening to my advice. Who he was a few days before was the sum total of his life. There would be no adjustments or additions except those manufactured by memory.

I looked at her and thought about perfect and imperfect days. It was loss of the imperfect days that scared me. Perfect days were remembered and treasured. The imperfect ones were taken for granted and forgotten. Until, there were no more.

"I love you," I said.

"I love you too."

"Will you marry me?"

She laughed. "You're proposing to me at a bar?"

"Yup."

"Where's the ring?"

I pulled the straw from her drink, fastened it into a loop, and slid it on her finger.

"You're so romantic."

"I love you. I want to marry you."

"When?"

I thought about it. "May twentieth."

She pulled out her phone and looked at the calendar.

"The next time May twentieth is on a Saturday is seven years from now."

"Perfect."

"Way to commit."

"Progress. Will you marry me?"

"Maybe." She kissed me.

We sat there until last call. I told her about Keegan: his brilliance, his flaws, his imperfections, his perfect humanity. I was sure that, in my former home just up the street, he was on the verge of sainthood. I wanted my son to be remembered as he really was; at least there at that moment. He made mistakes. He got up and brushed himself off. He did stupid things amid moments of genius. I was the wrong person for objective remembrance, but I tried. She had never met Keegan. I wanted her to understand him in all his imperfections and see his grace. I did not want him to be a perfect memory. He was a real person with real problems just like the rest of us. And he was good in spite of that.

"I might marry you," she said as we walked to the car. It was a cold and clear night. The stars glistened. I looked for Orion, but he had already set. She was still wearing her straw ring. She saw me looking up.

"Thank you for sharing Keegan with me."

I held her close and kissed the soft spot below her ear. We stood there for quite a while. I was afraid to let her go.

• • •

I hiked along watching Merlin's ponytail bounce. I stayed far enough back not to annoy him. I had been on the trail about two months. Riding in a car was strange. Watching television was a novelty. A hot shower was a treasure. I didn't know what congress was doing or who was in a pennant race. Clean underwear was sublime. I marked time by shadows and the sun. Most times I did not know what day of the week it was. The morning news was replaced with maps and a guidebook. My prism on the world had changed.

I wondered what Merlin's prism revealed after so many years of wandering. Did he know about tsunamis or earthquakes in other parts of the world? Did he care about wars being waged or the economy? He stooped to pull a plant from the ground, digging the root out carefully with his knife. He waved it in the air and grinned.

I couldn't decide about Merlin. I admired the joy he found in a tasty root. He was self-sufficient in his life of simplicity. He came and went at his whim, and he had friends happy to see him. He had created a pleasant life with nature, but was he a turtle who never left his shell? Was there defeat in choosing not to engage in the harsh realities of the world? Would Thoreau be as admired if he never left Walden Pond? Was it the path of least resistance? More importantly, did it matter? The heart of the matter was whether I would become a Merlin or something else. A Buttercup fluttered by, and I kept walking.

The trail was wide and straight at that point. The branches of the trees on either side mingled overhead. I walked with my thoughts in the long green tunnel. A thick wad of spider web was strung up to one side, and I stopped to watch thousands of baby spiders scurrying out of it. A blue jay was already eyeing them. I wondered how many would live through the day and how many would advance to spider old age. I didn't know how long a spider's life span was. I'd have to ask Merlin. When I was a boy I caught a black widow and kept it in a mason jar. I fed it crickets from the basement, and it lived through the winter. I released it in the spring. Life span is a cruel joke.

The trail dumped onto a gravel road. The sun and my stomach told me it was lunch time.

"There's a nice spot to eat just down the road here," Merlin said.

"Okay."

So, we took a right, me in the lead, and talked about spiders. Soon we arrived at manicured lawns and gardens and passed a sign that read

"Christ of the Mountain Retreat Center."

"Really?" I said.

A group of people were in a gazebo by a pond. We sat in the cool grass under a wide elm tree. I cooked ramen noodles with Tabasco sauce. Merlin ate nuts and berries.

A middle-aged priest walked toward us. He wore black, thick framed glasses and had a closely cropped hair cut. He walked with a straight back and a little swagger.

"Father," Merlin said and rose to shake his hand.

"Hello Merlin. Welcome back."

I stood, and Merlin introduced us. He was Father Norman. He ran the center, and they hosted spiritual retreats for couples, women and seniors.

"Polar was in the Army too."

"Where were you stationed?" the priest asked.

"Ft. Benning, Georgia."

"Infantry?"

"Yes sir."

"I went to airborne school there," he said.

We talked about falling out of airplanes. We were both five jump chumps; those who completed the five jumps required for graduation but then the Army never assigned to an airborne unit. He told me he had served in Germany, Korea, and Ft. Polk, Louisiana. I had always found military chaplains interesting. I didn't understand why a man who dedicated his life to religion would willingly join an organization whose essential purpose was to kill people.

"Are you staying with us for a while?" he asked.

"Have to ask him," I said, and I gestured toward Merlin who had wandered off to inspect a vegetable garden.

"We have some work to be done."

Father Norman explained that hikers would help out with repairs and maintenance at the center in exchange for meals and a place to pitch a tent. The priest went off to talk to Merlin. I leaned against the cool elm and watched them walk together. The ex-military man of god and the ponytailed vagabond made an interesting pair. Their conversation appeared to be heated; although I couldn't make out all the words. Eventually the priest made the sign of the cross over Merlin, and they made their way back toward me.

"Everything okay?" I asked.

"This one still thinks I need saving," Merlin said.

"I'll expect you in the spring," Father Norman said.

"I promised." Merlin lifted his pack. I sat down to pull on my boots.

"Are you going to help us out, Polar?" Father Norman asked.

I thought about it. I did owe God for a couple favors on this hike.

"I'll see you in Harper's Ferry," Merlin said. "You can get some churchin' up." He laughed.

"Asshole."

"Dickhead."

"Sorry, Father."

Merlin adjusted his straps and buckled up. "Careful with this one. He's worse than Frog, but he can keep a secret," he said to me.

"Go hike somewhere," the priest said.

I spent the afternoon prying rotted boards off a porch and replacing them with new two by sixes. The fresh pine smell mixed with that of decay. It reminded me of working on my dad's construction crew when I was a boy. He paid me twenty five cents an hour. The people on retreat came and went. Most seemed to have a stupid, vacant smile as if trying too hard to appear spiritual.

The full sun above was warm but not hot. Traveling south I had managed to stay just a little ahead of the change of seasons, but it was catching up. The breeze carried the distinct but unidentifiable air of change.

With the porch repair complete I went down to the pond. I peeled off my shirt and boots and waded in. A couple turtles sunning themselves on a log plopped into the water. Here and there a frog floated with just a head above the surface like a bump on the water. I swam out and drifted on my back and watched lazy clouds. A group of people were gathering in the gazebo up the hill. The men were in blazers and khakis. The women wore sundresses. I remembered when I wore blazers and khakis. A green gob of algae floated onto my chest. I left it there and enjoyed the coolness of the water.

I heard a whirring sound and looked up to see an old man in a motorized wheel chair at the edge of the pond. He was missing a leg and a hand and wore a blue baseball cap with gold trim common among those retired from the Navy.

"Bet that feels good," he said.

"Very much."

He scooted his chair so close to the edge that I worried he'd topple in. He looked at the water as if debating whether he might go for a swim as well. The church bells began to chime. That apparently helped him reach a resolution. He waved to me, backed up, and drove away.

I was sitting on the steps of the porch I had repaired earlier watching the sunset. The couples in blazers and sundresses had emerged from the chapel and reconvened in the gazebo to drink white wine. Father Norman came up the path and paused to look at the sinking sun.

"Another beauty," he said. He went inside and came back out with two tumblers of scotch on ice and sat down beside me.

"Thanks."

"I didn't see you at Mass."

"How do you know I'm Catholic?"

"Professional insight."

I smiled and raised my glass.

"When was the last time you went to Mass?"

"About twenty years ago."

"You'll be more work than Merlin. What's your story?"

"I'm just a hiker."

"Bullshit."

"I'm not here to be saved."

He gave me an appraising look as if he might call bullshit again. Instead he watched the gazebo people. We sat. The only sound was the occasional clink of ice or a laugh that carried from the gazebo. I enjoyed the drink. I had come to appreciate ice. I took note that Father Norman was not out mingling with the guests who wanted to be saved. When the sun was well out of sight he commented on the repairs to the porch and offered me a vacant cottage. I declined and asked where to pitch my tent.

I lifted my pack and decided I'd sleep by the pond. As I passed the gazebo a woman called out to me.

"Excuse me, sir. The air conditioning in our room is not working."

I paused.

"Say three Hail Mary's," I said, "and sleep naked." I heard them muttering about how even a retreat should have better help as I walked away.

The pond was a cacophony. Bullfrogs croaked. Cicadas and crickets played dueling banjos. Fish were rising and splashing. The birds were chirping their good nights. An owl called out his good morning. I put my feet in the water, leaned against a soggy log, and enjoyed the racket. After I was still for a few minutes, a muskrat emerged on the opposite bank. He reviewed his surroundings and set about gnawing through the underbrush. A snake, maybe a foot long, slapped against my leg as it wriggled through the water. I breathed in the heavy smells of loam and rot and wet; holding them in my lungs. I watched and listened, breathed and smelled. I could feel mud in my toes, water on my legs, wet grass beneath me and rotting wood against my back. The odors of loam and musk floated around me. I felt connected.

I slept until sunrise. At some point in the night I pulled my feet from the water and curled up on the muddy bank. I awoke to a wasp crawling on the dried and crusted mud on my arm. It must have been looking for building materials. Honey bees were getting about their day; barely staying airborne in the morning air. I waded into the pond, washed away the mud, and replaced it with a film of algae.

Bandana on my head, shirtless, and tinted with green, I set about the day's chores. The gazebo people were not yet awake, but I hammered loose boards and stomped on roofs as I cleared gutters. They began to emerge in sweats and robes. Father Norman came jogging up the gravel road. He wiped the sweat from his face with his shirt, checked his pulse, looked up at me and said, "We don't usually start this early," and then walked toward his cottage. I kept working.

At noon I sat under the big elm to eat my turkey sandwich. The gazebo people were returning from a half hour guided nature walk. Father Norman came from the garden and sat beside me.

"They're not bad people," he said. I shrugged. "You're a little judgmental."

"Just a little," I said, and I smiled.

"It seems to be a defense mechanism."

"Turkey *and* insights."

"It's a package deal." Now he smiled. We sat for a while watching the comings and goings. The gazebo people had an afternoon session on "sexuality and spirituality in marriage." It was being taught by a nun.

"Want an easier job for the afternoon?" he asked.

"Sure."

"Go for a walk with Ben."

"Who's Ben?"

Ben was the guy in the wheelchair. He was a retired accountant and helped them with the books. There was a packed sand and gravel loop trail out into the forest, but the priest worried about him being out alone.

"He has a lot of great stories. You might learn something." He got up and started to walk away.

"Polar?"

"Yeah?"

"Use of the showers is included in your stay."

I laughed.

"Cleansing is part of being saved," he said.

I thought about calling him an asshole.

• • •

I padded along in flip flops. Ben whirred beside me in his chair. The path snaked through trees. I thought that, if the trail were like this, I could crank serious mileage and considered that my prism had me evaluating walking conditions. We occasionally passed a plaque stuck into the ground to identify a plant. Any fauna that may have been about was alerted well in advance of our arrival by Ben's chair and the running commentary he maintained.

"I was on a battleship in the Korean war," he said. He lost his hand when a round he was loading into a big gun went off. Those big guns could fire from miles off shore. He lost his leg to diabetes. Accountants don't need legs or two hands; just one hand to run the ten key. He had his own little one-man accounting shop doing mostly tax work for small corporations until he retired nine years ago. It wasn't really one man because he had a secretary. A big plus of the chair was that it allowed him to go to the head of the buffet line. His wife died from ovarian cancer a year after he retired and they had moved to Florida. After she was gone, he came back up North to live.

It occurred to me that I was not there to ensure Ben's safety on the well ordered path. I was there for companionship, and to listen to him drone. I was annoyed, but I smiled and nodded.

We stopped at a small pond. It was completely choked with algae. A tern waded in the muck looking for fish that weren't there.

"Would you drink that?" he asked.

"Huh?"

"If you were thirsty enough?"

I thought about parking lot puddle water.

"Yeah, I'd drink that."

"Most people would die of thirst first."

We moved along until we came to a bench on the side of the path beneath a towering oak. Ben stopped his chair and said I probably needed a rest. We'd traveled about a half mile. I smiled and sat down. I leaned back and looked at the tree. It was a good old tree. Ben wondered aloud how old it was.

"Maybe a hundred years," I said.

"You know a lot about nature."

"Some. There are many who know a lot more."

"Good skill to have."

"Is it?" I asked.

We sat for a while. It was the first time he was quiet. I pulled out my knife and cut some mushrooms that were growing under the bench. I stuffed them in my cargo pocket.

"Ready to head back?" I asked.

"Let's do the whole loop." He gave the chair full throttle, and his tires spun a little in the gravel. I sighed.

We moved down the path. The forest darkened, and I looked at the sky. Thick, dark clouds were boiling above the tree tops.

"We're going to have weather," I said.

The wind kicked in, and there was a noticeable drop in temperature. I knew hail was coming. Fat drops of rain began to hit the ground and explode. Soon, we were in a deluge. Streams formed on the path, and it became a sandy soup.

"This is bad," Ben said.

"It will blow past."

His wheels were spinning. I could see that mud was clogging up his axle. The whir of the motor turned to a whine.

"This is *bad*," he said again. His eyes were wide. It was just a downpour, but I understood his fear. It was the fear of limitation. He was now completely stuck, and he was breathing heavily. Lightning cracked above.

"It's not so bad. I needed a shower." I pulled on his front wheel. My grip wasn't what it once was, but I managed to get the chair moving. It hurt like hell. The mud in the axle ate up most of the chair's horsepower. So, I pulled, he drove, and we got under the sheltering boughs of a pine tree just as the hail began to pelt down. Ben's hand had a white knuckle grip on the handlebar, and he was panting.

"We're okay. Just some hail."

"How will we get back? My chair doesn't go in mud." His voice was high pitched.

"We'll take a shortcut through the pond."

It didn't get a smile, but his eyes stopped darting around and focused on me. I offered him half of a granola bar.

"Tell me about your wife," I said, hoping to distract him from his fear.

He talked about meeting her in a history class in college. She had red hair and green eyes. They went to Disneyland on their honeymoon. She couldn't cook worth a damn, and wouldn't let him leave the house without pressing his shirt. She couldn't have children. They liked to play Scrabble, and she always won. I noticed his death grip on the handle bar had eased up. I pulled the water bottle out of the pouch on the back of his seat and handed it to him.

"Are you married?" he asked.

"I'm engaged." The hail was still crashing down.

"What's her name?"

"BSW." The occasional icy bomb burst through our sheltering tree and smacked us.

"Ouch. That's her name?"

I told him the story about how she came to be called the Beautiful Sunny Woman.

"But what's her name?"

"Penelope."

"Tell me about her."

So, I told him about her love of cheese, how she was incapable of spotting a moose a hundred yards away, how she could tie any knot, her sorting of spiders into "save it and put it outside" and "kill it, it's evil," her fear of flying and her fearlessness of just about everything else, and how beautiful she looked with dirt on her face.

"You love her very much." His breathing had slowed back to normal.

"Yes, I do."

"So why aren't you married?"

"It's complicated." Lightning hit near us and electrified the air. I felt the hair on my arms raise.

"Does she love you?"

"I hope so." I wondered what my absence was doing to our relationship. A roll of thunder shook the trees.

"Why?"

"Why do I hope so?"

"No, why does she love you?"

That was an interesting question. I thought about it and didn't have a good answer.

"I don't know. Just lucky, I guess."

"Yes, you are."

We watched the hail make a blanket of white on the ground. Then, just as quickly as it had come, the storm was spent and gone. The dark sky opened up to cornflower blue. Still, there was the matter of getting Ben and his chair back through the muck. He immediately sank to his axles when we left the shelter of the pine. I could see the fear return to his eyes. I pulled the compression straps off the back of his seat and fashioned a harness that I attached to his handlebars.

"Still want to do the whole loop?" I asked, but he didn't respond.

I leaned into the harness and pulled. I heaved, he steered, and we made slow progress. After a couple hundred yards I was dripping in sweat, and my quads were burning. In low spots on the path I had to get down on all fours and lunge to get the chair unstuck.

"Mush," Ben yelled. His mood had improved. I looked back at him, and he was smiling. Eventually we reached the pond. I collapsed on the bank. It was uphill to the main building. The stress on his motor in the mud had worn his battery down, but we still had one more stretch to go. After a few minutes' rest I rolled over and pulled the harness over my shoulder.

"Ready?" I asked.

"Let's do it."

I laughed at his use of "let's." I tilted forward and pulled. The wet grass was slick so I ended up crawling. The gazebo people watched us. I thought about flipping them off, but I was too fucking tired. About halfway up, Father Norman came. He wrapped his hand through the harness, pulled, and immediately slipped and fell. His clean black suit was muddy and green. Grass was stuck to his face and white collar. He grinned, and we pulled.

"Good workout," he said. I guzzled water from the hose.

"We were nearly trapped out there," Ben said. I was behind him and shook my head. Ben told the story of the storm and the hail and the mud. It was almost biblical in his telling. I smiled and thought it would be embellished many more times.

"Quite an adventure," Father Norman said. I put my thumb on the end of the hose and began to spray the mud and muck off myself.

"You need a trail name after an experience like that," I said.

"A trail name?"

"We'll call you Wheels."

"Wheels. I like that," Ben said.

"Well, Wheels, I need to go change my clothes," Father Norman said. One of the nuns came by and offered to push Ben to his room. The priest smiled at me.

That evening I sat on the porch with my feet propped on the railing and watched the sun drift away. My thighs were still quivering from the workout. I had an idea how sherpas felt. I sipped the glass of scotch the priest had brought me. Ben came whirring around the corner, his chair washed and recharged. He pulled up next to me.

"Hey Wheels."

He handed me a pocket watch. It was silver and tarnished and intricately engraved.

"What's this?" I asked.

"Thank you for not leaving me."

I was about to ask who would have done such a thing, but I stopped. The world was full of people who leave. I looked at the watch and ran my finger over the ornate case.

"I can't accept this."

He explained that it was his grandfather's. The railroad company had given it to him at his retirement. He had no children and wanted me to have it.

"Well...thank you." I still didn't feel that I should take it. More importantly, I didn't want it.

Fireflies were emerging down by the pond. They flashed and flickered. There was the glow of lightning beyond the horizon. Another storm was pushing in.

"Can I offer you some advice?" Ben asked.

"Sure."

"When you get home, you marry that girl. And don't take too long getting home."

I was silent.

"Plenty of regrets in this life. That shouldn't be one of them."

• • •

After another day of assorted labor, I figured I was squared up with God. I was eager to catch up to Merlin. Pack loaded, I drank coffee with Father Norman. He had just come back from his morning run. It reminded me of seeing my priest skiing when I was about twelve. It just seemed incongruous. He offered to hear my confession, and I laughed; perhaps a little too harshly.

"Whatever your issues with God, he loves you."

I didn't say anything.

"Is being angry at God also part of your defense mechanism?"

"Still not here to be saved."

"Where then? Will you be saved out in the woods? Or are you just hiding out there?"

"Maybe," I said, aware that there were two questions.

Father Norman smiled. "The peace you find out there?" and he gestured toward the wood line. "Still God."

I shrugged and sipped my coffee. A pair of hummingbirds flitted about the flowers. I liked the priest and decided not to share my opinions of his god. Ben came cruising up the path and looked at my pack.

"Leaving us?" he asked.

"Yup."

"Well, be careful out there. And remember what I said. It's a beautiful day for a walk. Let's pray." I sighed and bowed my head while he asked God to watch over my journey. We shook hands, and he whirred off to inventory an arriving food delivery.

"That wasn't so bad," the priest said.

"Just humoring an old man."

"Careful. Someone might think you care."

"Funny."

"I like seeing Merlin arrive here because I know he's always out there wandering."

"How's the saying go? All who wander are not lost." I hoisted my pack and adjusted the straps.

"That implies some are." He fingered his rosary. "Polar?"

"Yeah?"

"I hope I never see you again." He gave me a benediction, we shook hands, and I walked into the forest.

• • •

I was back among the familiar sights and sounds of the woods. Birds called in the canopy, and small things scurried in the brush. Bushwhacking southeast up and over a couple hills, I rejoined the AT. The ringing church bells lingered in the morning air like a reminder. I hopped over a deadfall and opened up my stride. At two and a half to three miles an hour, I could walk all day. I whistled as I hiked.

The priest's understanding of me was irritating. As with Frog, he seemed to look right into me. Even Merlin seemed to have me pegged. Perhaps I wore some invisible hair shirt or scarlet letter to identify me to those looking. Still, they found something of worth as they peered so I had that going for me.

My pack was light, and I felt strong. For many, hiking the AT was a war of attrition. They were eroded each day and just hoped to reach their destination while there was still something of them left. It was having the opposite effect on me. I skipped across rocks and balanced on logs. Pausing silently in the shadow of a tree trunk, it was only a short time until I was rewarded with sight of a raccoon. The sun was reaching its zenith. Being nocturnal, he was up late going about his raccoon business. He stopped to examine something with his little people-like hands.

When he had scampered up a fallen tree with his bouncy gait, I continued on my way. It was thirty miles to Harper's Ferry. Possible to do in a day, but I'd take two and enjoy the walk. I wondered what Merlin was doing; probably bitching to someone or about something. I thought about the characters I had met so far on my journey. I wondered how close Ajax was to Katahdin. His similarity to Keegan assured me he'd make it. How far had Treadmore gone who, it seemed so long ago, had encouraged me to hike my own hike? I pictured Three Miles and Frog sitting in their Adirondack chairs with assorted members of the tribe. Ben was probably still counting loaves of bread, and Father Norman was herding gazebo people. I hoped Plumber's Crack and the mute were out on the trail today.

Each had altered my journey in some way. As such, each had altered at least the history of me. I stopped to watch chipmunks hauling acorns into a log. What was the alteration? Was it significant and noticeable or infinitesimal? I supposed only time and distance would tell. The chipmunks discovered my observation and halted their work, perhaps afraid I had learned of their secret stash. I moved on.

I came to a quiet brook. I could see from the map that it meandered around a hill. The trail crossed it, went over the hill and bisected it again on the other side. I decided to follow the brook. Through hikers were obligated to stay on the trail to "complete" it. I remained a meanderer.

People came and went in all lives. How often did we recognize the imprint they left behind? I splashed along in the shallow water; occasionally disturbing a frog as I went. Hucka, who read Keegan's eulogy for me, and I were really all who were left from our childhood circle of friends. If not for a poor calculation of body mass and chemical requirements on my part, he'd be the only one. Sellers, my old climbing partner, committed suicide after his third failed marriage, a second failed business venture and bankruptcy. Matt overdosed on coke when he was twenty-three. Tommy died of cancer when we were twenty-five. Todd was in a horrific accident on a dirt bike. He remained alive, but the brain damage left only a shell of the person he once was.

I climbed the wet bank to go around the deep pool of a beaver pond. I sat quietly for a while hoping to see one, but none showed, and I continued on. Considering the events of my own life, it seemed I had learned little from those I knew from early on. Was it reasonable to expect impact from brief encounters? Perhaps receptiveness played a role. Letting an inchworm in the middle of a patch of rocks crawl onto my finger so I could move him to a leaf, I was reminded of the BSW. She once stopped the car in traffic to get an inchworm off the windshield and take him to a shrub.

The brook circled the hill, and I rejoined the trail. A couple of day hikers were sitting on the foot bridge when I came splashing up the brook. I offered a good afternoon, filled a water bottle, pulled on my boots, and went up the trail as they stared at me. It wasn't until later that I realized someone emerging from the forest and hiking barefoot up the middle of a creek might seem a bit odd. I hiked and thought about my relationships with my father and my remaining son. I certainly had my role, but perhaps I was not the sole cause of the rancor. I brushed a spider web from my face and leaned in as I worked my way up and out of the valley.

The ridgeline was lit with the warm glow of the late afternoon sun. I stopped to take some pictures. I rarely remembered to do that. I had less than twenty pictures from the six hundred some odd miles I had walked. It didn't bother me much. I had my journal for memories, and I had sights, smells, and sounds seared into my brain. Bits of fluff from cottonwood trees drifted in the air like a premonition of snow.

I had covered about nineteen miles. Although there were still a few hours of daylight, it was a good spot to camp, and the next day would be easy at eleven or twelve miles anyway. I kicked off my boots and propped my feet up for their moment. I had stared up at a lot of trees. Just like the sunlight that was melting away, the clarity and insights of the day dissolved. Still, they had come. Perhaps they'd come again. Perhaps they'd linger.

The skies were clear so I strung my groundcover up as a lean-to between a couple trees instead of putting up the tent, and I set off into the meadow to look for vegetables. I found some burdock, and I dug up the roots. I also found what I thought was chickweed, but it is too similar to its poisonous cousin so I left it alone. I sliced the roots thin then boiled them with pasta, added some salmon and topped it off with Tabasco sauce.

I slurped my dinner from the pot and had a Hershey bar for dessert. Leaning against a Poplar, I carved the Appalachian Trail logo onto my stick and watched a few hikers go by trying to squeeze more mileage out of the day. I smiled and waved out of obligation. I could see possibly hiking the whole trail if it happened by accident; if I just kept walking and one day arrived at the end. Setting out from point A to get to point B didn't interest me. A previous version of me would have been hell bent on that accomplishment. I wasn't sure how I felt about that. I carved some more and blew the shavings to the ground. They would be good squirrel nest material.

The stars came out. I waited for Orion to lift above the trees then crawled under my shelter.

• • •

It was the ugliest dog I had ever seen. It had one snaggle tooth that stuck up out of its closed mouth. The eyes were milky and didn't aim the same direction. Its wiry black hair extended in all directions from the protozoa shaped body. It lay in our yard with one eye watching us. The other seemed to be looking at the fence.

"Ohhh, are you lost?" the BSW asked it. It whimpered and then snarled but did not move when she approached it. I sighed. Before she could ask, I handed her one of the hot dogs I was preparing to grill, and she fed the little creature.

"She doesn't have a collar," she said as she scratched behind its ears. I looked up at the orange leaves on the oak trees. The japanese maple's had turned deep, crimson. Penny carried the little dog into the house. I sat down on the patio and opened a beer. Our dogs in the house began barking about the visitor.

Two beers later she emerged with the thing wrapped in a towel. The bath had not improved its appearance. The camera dangled from her wrist.

"Here. Hold her," she said and held the dog toward me. It snapped at me. Penny took its picture and went back in the house. I sat holding the growling little thing.

We spent the afternoon putting up "Dog found" signs around the neighborhood. Animal control did not have any reports of a lost dog fitting its description. Penny posted a notice on Craig's list.

"I'll have to take her to the vet in the morning to have her checked out," she said.

"Why don't we just take her to the pound?" I asked although I already knew the answer. Our three dogs and the new arrival were racing around the backyard and fighting over chew toys. One of our cats watched them with disdain from atop the fence.

After a week and a second trip to the vet to treat a uterine tract infection, nobody had called to claim the ugliest dog in the world. I didn't even know dogs could get uterine tract infections. We sat at the kitchen table drinking coffee. The dogs were all trying to decide who had the best breakfast. She had been named Lucy, and she was in the midst of the scrum. The cats were sprawled about the kitchen floor. I could hear the rabbit hopping about in its hutch. Penny watched the menagerie and smiled. She was the keeper of needful things. Not all were pets.

. . .

So, I spent the morning following a lizard. It was small, about the size of an index finger, a variegated green and with a tail longer than its body. He dashed from rock to rock; pausing to swivel an eyeball back at me. After an hour or so, I concluded lizards really don't have any place they need to be or secrets to tell, and I wandered back to my camp. I liked the inconsequential moments the trail gave me.

It was a beautiful morning; just a bit warmer than chilly and with clear skies. I ate my oatmeal and gazed about. Perhaps I *could* find my answers out here. Of course, I still wasn't even sure of the questions. I considered how much a medicine bottle full of brown sugar might weigh. It would improve the oat meal. I had four bars on my phone so I called the BSW.

"Hey Puppy Chow," she said. After I had explained the concept of trail names to her, she had decided to call me that.

"Hey Shit head."

"Hey!"

"How's things on the home front?"

"We have lots of squash, and a pumpkin bigger than a basketball." We had planted a garden in the spring.

"Don't pick it yet."

"I'm not. When are you coming home to see it?"

I had been waiting for that question. It was the first time she asked it.

"I don't know."

"I miss you."

"I miss you too."

There was a period of quiet on the phone.
"Honey?" I asked.
"Yes?"
"Why do you love me?"
She laughed. "That's a dumb question."
"I'm not asking *if* you love me. I'm asking why."
She paused, and I watched a pair of ducks that had come to rest in the glade.
"Because you're almost as smart as I am. You're clever. You're funny when you want to be. You're usually kind. You have a strong sense of ethics. You stand up for what you think is right. You love your children in a way many dads don't. You give me flowers for no reason. You let me choose which side of the bed to sleep on. You're a better cook than me. You accomplish what you set out to do. I'm happy when I'm around you. I can't picture my life without you. Even when beating yourself up, you strive to be a good person. Want me to keep going?"
"That'll do, pig. Thank you."
"Shut up. Why do you ask? Need a mid-trail ego boost?"
"Nah. Just curious."
"I love you."
"I love you too," and I said it with as much conviction as I ever had. Ben, my physical albatross, had a point. I was still dealing with the metaphorical ones. Perhaps I was making progress.

• • •

I read a lot about Kit Carson, Jim Bridger and such when I was a boy. While my friends wanted to play cowboy, I wanted to be a mountain man. Somewhere, I still had the coonskin cap I got at Yellowstone and wore the entire summer that I was ten. The mountain men would descend and gather to sell their pelts, resupply and let loose among civilization they avoided most of the year. Harper's Ferry was such a place for hikers; except hikers aren't escaping hostile natives and have convenience stores every twenty miles. It was a small town built into the cut bank of a river, the headquarters of the Appalachian Trail Conservancy, and people with packs are as common as the tourists waddling its streets.

After a three mile walk along an old canal road, I crossed a rickety bridge and entered hiker central in the early afternoon. A couple of NoBo's high fived me as we passed. I was aiming for the outfitter figuring they would know Merlin, but I didn't make it past the first bar.

"Hey Polar!" A guy I did not know yelled from an open window. I looked at him, confused.

"Polar. C'mon," he yelled again and waved me to come in.

He met me at the door of the bar and helped me off with my pack. I could see the place was filled with hikers and tourists who had come to see the Civil War sights and natural beauty.

"I'm Stellar," he said.

"Good. I'm okay."

"No, I'm called Stellar."

"Do I know you?"

"Merlin told us to watch for you. Short guy, red pack, good boots, bandana, carved stick."

I laughed as Stellar ushered me to a table, and I met more of my tribe. There was Stellar's twin brother, Famous. Two women with crew cuts, holding hands, were introduced as Pantsless Jack and the Skinny Chick. A guy who looked like a tax accountant was called Rage. I shook hands all around, and Famous handed me a glass of beer from the several pitchers on the table. I sat and took a long, satisfying drink.

"Where's Merlin?" I asked.

"He has a friend in town," Rage said and made quotations with his fingers when he said "friend."

"Good for him," I said.

"Frog's told us all about you," Skinny Chick said.

"That can't be good."

"Welcome to the tribe!" Pantsless Jack said.

There was a round of toasts. I told them about the retreat center and Father Norman, whom they all seemed to know. Stellar explained that Rage was a dotcom millionaire on his third through hike, and they made him pay for everything. Rage explained that Stellar and Famous were hackers ripping off his company among others to finance spending their summers on the trail. Pantsless Jack and Skinny Chick were getting ready to start their fourth hike of Virginia. They hadn't done any other part of the trail because they liked that one so much.

Although I mostly sat back and listened, I did offer a story now and then. I felt comfortable with this group of people I had just met. Several more pitchers were polished off. The sun was dipping, and I asked where we were sleeping. Famous told me they were at a hostel two doors down, but they were wall to wall. There was another hostel a mile up the road. I was a little disappointed, but I had trained myself to situate a sleeping spot. So, I hoisted my pack and promised to be back in a little while.

"Hey Polar," Skinny Chick called. I turned back.

"Welcome to the tribe," she said, and she gave me a strangely sincere and serious look.

I went out the door and up the main street. It was crowded, and I weaved my way. Several families stopped me to ask where I was going and how far I'd come. One family, a mother with three children, had a little boy in a coonskin cap. It still had the tag. He reached out to touch my walking stick.

"Do you like the woods?" I asked.

"Yes sir," he said with a southern drawl.

"Get out in the woods every chance you get. That's what Daniel Boone did." His mother smiled at me and said he was afraid of meeting a bear.

"Do you know what to do when you see a bear?" I asked.

"No, sir."

"Run and scream like your little sister."

He laughed, and I explained that black bears were afraid of him and how to make himself look big to scare them even more. The mother laughed, thanked me, and asked if I'd like to join them for dinner to tell them more about adventures in the wilderness; her treat. Odysseus had his sirens too.

"Thank you, but I need to go find a place to sleep," and I walked up the street.

The hostel, as it were, was really a couple's house. There were four beds in the living room, and the only shower was upstairs in their bedroom. I tromped out in a bath towel and met the husband. He extended a hand, but I decided to hold up the towel. They were both world class kayakers, and they showed me videos of some of their insane drops. I was apparently the only one who found it weird that I was standing in a towel.

Back in the living room, I found two hikers. It was their first night, and they were starting out in the morning; aiming south and hoping to reach Springer. I remembered my first day and how utterly fucked up I was.

They introduced themselves as Bob and Nathan, in their early thirties and working on the bucket list as they called it.

"Your packs are too heavy," I said.

"How do you know?" Bob asked.

"You have a pot carabiner'ed to the outside."

We went through their packs, and I tossed unnecessary shit into a pile. It included speakers for an ipod, extra blankets, mittens, and a quart of olive oil.

"We want to enjoy the hike," Nathan said.

"You will, and you won't need that stuff."

They huddled considering whether to listen to me and what to do with the shit if they did.

"You guys want to talk to some real hikers?" I asked.

"What are you?"

"I'm just a meanderer."

• • •

We tromped down Main Street toward the hostel in the center of town. Lights glowed through windows, and I wondered what shows the people inside were watching. A fat couple with ice cream cones passed us. Inside the hostel was like a frat house with wool socks. Stellar was at the front door and hugged me. Bob, Nathan and I were handed red plastic cups of beer, and we worked our way in.

"Polar!" It was Famous. He was very drunk.

"Who are these guys?" he asked and spilled his beer on Bob.

"They're new hikers."

"This is a tribe party." He slurred the words as he pushed Nathan back. Bob and Nathan looked scared.

"Maybe you should get some air," I said. He looked at me for a moment as if debating the idea, slapped Bob on the back and stumbled toward the door.

"Nice crowd," Nathan said.

"They grow on you."

Bob and Nathan stopped to listen to a conversation about camp stoves, and I moved on looking for Merlin. Upstairs I passed a crowded room and a voice called out.

"Asshole."

"Dickhead," I called back from the hall. I worked my way in and found Merlin holding court. I was introduced to many more of the tribe. One woman offered me condolences about my son. I looked at Merlin.

"Talk to Frog," he said.

"How are you, old man?"

"You get some churchin'?"

"Asshole."

"Dickhead."

We smiled and shook hands. Outside the window I saw a blinking light, like a little LED. I looked closer and saw it was a firefly caught in a spider's web. It jerked and blinked as the spider worked on it, and it died.

A young woman with a long, blonde braid brought Merlin a beer. I grinned.

"Tough life," I said.

"What can I say? They worship me." That was greeted by a round of boos, fuck you's and laughter.

I told Merlin about my time at the retreat center, and he called it "good penance work." I was sitting next to him. Having not seen him for a few days, I noticed he appeared even thinner than usual.

"You okay?"

"I'm fine. Just need another beer."

"That's not what I meant."

"Not here."

I watched him as he discussed sections of trail and water sources with assorted members of the tribe. They were quick to include me. Many of them were heading North and wanted to hear about my journey. I shared the discovery and location of Guido Spring which seemed to impress everyone but Merlin, but I didn't feel as comfortable as I had expected; as I had looked forward to.

I wandered back downstairs and outside. Bob and Nathan were on the sidewalk making plans to hook up with a couple SoBo's in the morning.

"This was great, Polar! Thanks."

"No worries. Have a good hike," I said.

"When are you heading out?"

"Not sure. A day or two."

"Well, if we don't see you...."

"I'll catch you," I said. They wandered up the street to a bar with their new hiking buddies. I didn't think they'd be making much of a start the next day. I might catch them my first day out of Harper's Ferry.

I sat on the curb and watched the comings and goings of hikers and tourists. There was such a marked disparity between the two, and I was clearly in the former camp. I wondered what the BSW was doing and how our garden was holding up. Skinny Chick came out and sat beside me.

"Nice night," she said. I looked up at the clear sky and the stars that managed to work through the ambient light.

"Yeah." We watched an obese family go by on the other side of the street. The kids whined to go in a gift shop to buy inflatable swords, and the father commented about spending more god damn money.

"Is that you?" she asked.

"What?"

"In the real world, is that you?"

"I hope not."

She gave me an appraising look; weighing my merits.

"I see why Merlin likes you," she said.

"Beyond that I tolerate him, why is that?"

"Looking in a mirror."

I didn't say anything. I looked at how my flip flop was about to come undone. She stood up.

"Frog said to remind you not to get lost."

Pantsless Jack came out, and they walked away holding hands. I wandered back toward my hostel, passing a hiker puking in the street. The darkened homes seemed distant and forbidding.

• • •

Bob and Nathan stumbled in drunk and loudly early in the morning. It was a little before dawn, and I was already awake when they entered. When they were snoring I rose, slipped into my flip flops and padded out into the dark. There was a 7-11 a couple miles up the road, and I figured I could get a cup of shitty coffee there at that hour.

"You're getting an early start," the clerk at the convenience store said as I paid for my coffee and chocolate doughnut.

"Yeah."

"You NoBo or SoBo?"

"South."

"Have a good hike."

I smiled recalling I had said that to Merlin the first time we met and his reaction to it. Outside, I sat and leaned against the building. The vigil of the night was better with a doughnut. Grey crept into the sky at the horizon. A whippoorwill sang from the dark beyond the fluorescent lights. The BSW often asked what I thought about while I was awake at night. I thought about everything; my kids, events of my life, who invented spray cheese and why, and such. However, it was with a detachment not present during normal waking hours. While I was certainly conscious, it's like my brain wasn't fully operating. Maybe one lobe took a while to warm up. I called it unsleeping.

A homeless man entered the parking lot pushing a shopping cart. It was filled with what I would have called junk, but I realized each item was as essential to him as everything I carried in my pack. Really, little separated us except for perspective, and I probably had more expensive junk in my version of a shopping cart. I went inside and bought another coffee and more doughnuts.

He approached me silently with a cup held out. I offered him a coffee and the doughnuts. He hesitated then accepted. I put my change and ten dollars in his cup, and he sat down beside me. He smelled of body odor and dirt. It wasn't really different from the hiker stench I was accustomed to. We sipped our coffees and quietly waited for sunrise. When the first gleam shot across the sky, he rose, nodded to me, and set off pushing his cart. I wondered where he was going.

I wandered around town as it woke up and prepared for the day. Delivery men wheeled cases of beer and food into restaurants. Park Service swept out the historical display buildings. A commuter train came through taking its contents to DC. I read plaques explaining the journey of Lewis and Clarke. I got another cup of coffee from a café in town and went to sit by the river.

Merlin found me skipping rocks across the water.

"You stalking me?" I asked.

"It's a small town. I figured you'd be the only hiker not actually in town."

We skipped rocks for a while. Far out on the river a hawk dropped but came up clinging only water.

"What's up with you?" I asked.

"Just tired."

I watched him.

"You're buggin' me."

"You sure?"

"Yeah." He said he was turning back north and would spend a few months with Three Miles and Frog to rest up and drive away their customers.

We walked along the banks talking about the plants we found. I caught a frog, and he jumped in my closed hands, bouncing against my palms. I put him back in the water.

"What do you think of the tribe?" he asked.

"Like any group of people, it has its good and bad."

"True, but we call it a tribe; not a group or collective or any other word."

"Okay."

"The difference is any one of them will do anything to help. Skinny Chick will give you her last dime. Gizmo is a crazy fuck. He'd kill someone if you asked him. One of 'em might beat the shit out of a guy in a grocery store for you."

I didn't say anything, and we walked a while. Merlin found some wild mint, and we chewed on the leaves.

"You're not used to that, are you?"

"What?"

"People you can count on."

"The BSW...."

But he cut me off.

"I think it's a given in a good relationship. I mean just friends, or even just acquaintances."

We walked some more. The sun was warm, and the water chattered beside us.

"No," I said.

We made our way up the hill on oak lined streets to a small clapboard house with a covered porch. A Jeep, Subaru, and a van covered with stickers were parked in front. There was a canoe and a kayak with a broken hull in the yard and some fly rods stacked up against a front window. It was Frog's house without the retail and her whimsy.

"Mellower than last night," Merlin said.

Famous met me in the yard and apologized. I told him it was no big deal. He put his arm around my shoulders and steered me toward the beer cooler.

"Kicked the shit out of a guy in the frozen foods," he said. "That's awesome."

Stellar was playing James Taylor and Jack Johnson songs on guitar. Famous left to pick up a banjo and join him. Pantsless Jack and Skinny Chick were making out on a rocking chair. A couple women in ankle length skirts and long braids danced in that crunchy, granola, spastic sort of way. The mellow vibe reminded me of the time with Three Miles and Frog.

Rage, in a Hawaiian shirt, came and sat by me. We talked about Guido Springs and how cool it was that I had found a spring. He said he would have named it after himself. I said I considered naming it Eponymous Spring, but the toad deserved the credit. He didn't get the joke. We compared notes on places we'd both hiked.

A heavyset man in Carhartt pants and steel toed boots approached. I stood up to shake hands. He was Festus, and it was his house. He'd been out clearing deadfall off the trail. I thanked him for having me.

"Anyone who fights for Merlin is alright in my book," he said. I nodded embarrassed.

"You need a place to stay, right?" he asked.

"I'm up at the other hostel."

"That place is a shithole. You come stay here. When you headin' out?"

"I think tomorrow."

"Our scrapper's on a mission." He and Rage laughed.

I did not want to be known for a fight, but it seemed too late. He called his teenage son over, and despite my protests, sent him to get my pack and boots from the hostel.

"Thank you."

I found it curious how everyone knew so much about me, and I knew almost nothing about them.

"Any time you want the news, call Frog or Daisy. She's down south, and you ain't met her yet," Festus said.

"Frog was sending emails two minutes after you hiked out her door," Rage said.

"I'm that big a news?"

"Yes," they said almost in unison.

"Why?"

"There's about fifty or sixty members of our tribe. Merlin and Three Miles really started it. You're the first new member Merlin's ever brought in."

I looked across the yard at Merlin. He was supervising the barbecue. Was I an apprentice? Grumpy, old, loner bastard in training?

Festus' son returned with my gear.

"Tent or bed?" Festus asked me.

"I'll take the bed."

"Good man." And he ordered his son to haul it up to the spare room. Skinny Chick had wandered over to join us.

"Our rock star new member," she said.

I looked at her and weighed my words. I recognized they would change things an awful lot. I'd probably have to find a place to sleep. She beat me to the punch.

"I'm kidding you, Polar. But you're still our rock star." She gave me a smile that seemed almost sympathetic.

There was a palpable deflation of tension. Rage laughed nervously. Famous and Stellar's music carried in the afternoon air. Festus shuffled his feet as if not sure whom he should stand closer to.

"I'm just a hiker," I said.

"You're not. Nobody is *just* a hiker."

"Maybe I'll be the first."

She raised her drink, and we clinked bottles. Rage and Festus took the opportunity to go inspect the barbecue. She laughed.

"Couple a brave ones there. Polar, don't get lost."

"I don't know what that means."

"For you? I don't either. I know it sounds cheesy, but when you figure out where you're going, stay on your trail."

"Profound."

"Fuck you."

"Thank you." We touched bottles again, and she went to find Pantsless Jack. I sat in the grass and considered all the people who knew how I should go, but none knew where. Since I didn't know, I guess I couldn't expect them to, but the well meaning concern was getting annoying.

Still, I had chosen to be there. I could have hiked on through. I thought of the firefly in the spider's web. As usual when I was around people, thoughts of the BSW and my kids floated across my mind.

Merlin came over and eased onto the grass beside me.

"What's up?" he asked.

"Tired of the good intentioned."

"They mean well."

"That's why I called them good intentioned."

"Yeah, it sucks having people concerned about you." He lay back in the grass and closed his eyes. He looked tired so I didn't ask the question.

He soon began to snore. I looked at him, how old and frail he really was. Awake and hiking, he was wiry and curmudgeonly. There, he seemed nearly dead; the snores being the only thing that kept me from wanting to shake him.

I lay back on the grass next to him and watched the deepening sky. I was somehow reluctant to leave his side. Perhaps irrationally, I was worried about missing some final moment. I knew what it was like to miss final moments. The other members of the tribe left us alone, and it was the dark end of twilight when he awoke. He lifted his head, saw me still next to him, paused and nodded at me, mumbled about the bathroom and wandered inside.

"You care for him," Skinny Chick said from a folding lawn chair off to my side.

"Yeah, I guess I do."

"You're a good man, Polar."

People often told me that. Others called me a complete asshole.

・・・

Festus was an early riser. That is, he was up when I was used to a couple more hours of solitary unsleeping. I went downstairs when I heard him start the coffee maker. He nodded at me and handed me a cup. I nodded back. We sat at his kitchen table and drank our coffee in silence. Festus was okay. I liked almost anyone who didn't talk much. Around dawn, Merlin came in the front door.

"Didn't want to miss you," he said as he poured himself a cup. The three of us then sat in silence sipping coffee. A rooster crowed somewhere, and Festus said he needed to get to work. I thanked him, he wished me well, and he left.

"Let's go outside," Merlin said.

We filled our cups and wandered down to the river in the dim light. We disrupted a nesting gaggle of geese on the bank. They honked their disapproval, and we retreated to a spot further downstream.

"You're not here to take care of me, if that's what you think," he said. I sat on a stump.

"Am I here to replace you?"

He laughed.

"You are a cocky one, but I'll give you credit for trying not to be. Besides, I ain't going anywhere."

"Then why am I here?"

He cut some mushrooms he found on the side of a log, sliced them and offered me a handful. I had not seen them before, but I popped one in my mouth.

"You're hiking to escape and to find answers. I'm not sure you can do both. You'll have to choose. I made my choice long ago."

"Maybe, but not what I meant."

"I know." He dug some roots from the wet soil near the water.

"Because I hope you'll decide to seek answers. That's why you're here." He handed me the roots. "Cook these with your tuna."

We walked and talked. He told me about the day his wife and son were killed. He told me about the day after. He told me about a year and then ten years after; all spent hiking, walking, moving, and trying to stay ahead of the memories. We talked about the pain and loss. We talked about the rage and unfairness. He did not try to console or advise me; nor me him. We just shared a common, horrific experience.

We watched the sun rise with our feet in the cold, rushing water. I thought that the talk we had was one I would have liked to have had with my father. I hadn't thought of him for a long time. He was somewhere in Mexico, and I hoped he was doing well. I wondered if Duncan considered that his dad was somewhere on the AT. I wondered if he hoped I was doing well.

"You're okay, old man."

"You're an asshole."

I knew my line, but I didn't say it.

We hiked back up to Festus' place. I put Merlin's roots in a plastic bag and buried them in the middle of the pack where they would stay cooler. I noticed some fraying on the pack. Just a few months ago, it had been brand new. It was a good shell. I pulled on my boots and laced them tightly. I filled my water bladder. Finally, there was nothing to do except walk. I lifted my pack and noticed my sea grass rope was gone. I looked around frantically.

Merlin handed it to me. He had re-woven it, and it was a tight, coiled cord.

"Thank you." I carefully fastened it to a loop on the pack.

He followed me back out to the trailhead. We stopped at the trail conservancy headquarters, and I had my picture taken. They made it into postcards that I sent to Quinn and the BSW. At the trailhead, several hikers were preparing to set off in the mid-morning. They snapped pictures and heaved up their overstuffed packs. Merlin and I walked a ways off the trail. We saw a praying mantis devour a spider.

"That's a fuckin' metaphor," he said.

"You said that before."

"I say it every time I see that."

"Well, I know all your tricks now."

"Not even close."

We stood in silence for a few minutes.

"Thank you, old man, for everything."

"You're welcome."

There was nothing to do except walk. I looked at a fern unfurling its leaves for the morning. A robin chirped above. The sun flickered through the canopy. A dog barked somewhere.

I held out my hand. Merlin held it. I hugged him, and he seemed a bit surprised.

"Thank you," I said.

"You know how to find me."

"Yup."

I turned and walked into the woods and wiped my eyes, afraid I would not see him again as so often happened. People leave.

. . .

I rose out of Harper's Ferry's water cut valley. The overcast sky whispered of rain. There were mushrooms in my pack for dinner, and the quiet rustle of forest noises followed me: a chirp, a trill, the creak of trees. A spider hitched a ride for a while on my stick. Poplars and cottonwoods dusted the air with their pollen and clouded the clean smell of ferns. I walked with my head high to gaze at all around me. Where the trail crested the ridge there was an old cemetery. A handful of graves were marked by eroded stones. A couple day hikers were having a picnic in their midst.

"Nice day," one said as I approached. He was wearing black Converse hightops. He was not a hiker.

"It is." I paused to take a sip of water.

"Where you headed?" the other asked. She had a tattoo of a sun covering most of her leg and enormous breasts that would have benefited from a sports bra.

"SoBo," I said, and added, "Southbound," when they looked at me with confusion.

I nibbled at a granola bar and tossed a few crumbs for the chipmunks waiting expectantly.

"Have a good hike," I said and moved on thinking about Merlin's reaction when I said that to him.

I walked slowly that day; taking time to wander off trail in pursuit of roots or to hunt for the secrets of snakes. Still, in late afternoon I had covered about seventeen miles. That section of trail was gullied with erosion and deadfalls sprawled across. In the absence of care, the forest would quickly reclaim the trail. There was still some time before day turned into night. I stood quietly in the dappled shade of young trees. I fingered the coil of my seagrass rope and looked at the dilapidated trail.

It needed some love.

Camp that night was in soft loam beneath a half dead oak. The mushrooms, sautéed in packets of soy sauce boosted from a Chinese restaurant, were delicious. I propped my bare feet on a chunk of granite and thought about that neglected section of trail. Elsewhere, it was lovingly stewarded. The shelters were clean and freshly painted. Often there was the treat of toilet paper in the privy. One even had baskets of hanging annuals. While I didn't like that intrusion, I appreciated the care.

The next day I retraced my steps a couple miles to a particular hill. The trail was washed out in many places there and deep ravines carved it. Brush invaded from the sides, and trees dumped unwanted parts. I stooped and lifted a log that sprawled across the path. It was about eight inches in diameter but lifted easily. It was rotted from the inside out. It had been there a while. I tossed it to the side.

I spent the morning moving logs and cutting away intrusive branches. With a flat slab of granite, a stick and some rope, I fashioned a crude shovel and set to work on grading and excavating. I used my hands more than I used the tool which a caveman Finn would have laughed at. Good dirt clogged my fingernails. On my hands and knees, I moved in the smell of newly turned earth.

After a few hours, I surveyed my work. The small bit of trail, perhaps fifty yards, was reclaimed. In contrast to its neighboring sections, it looked like it had a fresh coat of paint. Running against common sense, maintaining the two thousand mile scar lessens human impact. A clear, navigable trail attracts the masses like bugs to a light and keeps their influence confined. I recalled the trail magic chili dogs so many miles ago and was pleased with how I had given something back to the trail.

A lone hiker came through while I had been digging. He paused just long enough to take a drink of water.

"Thank you for your work," and he moved on. I smiled and wondered how Plumber's crack and the mute were doing. They had power tools. I had a rock tied to a stick.

I stripped in a trickling brook and washed away the sweat and grime. I scrubbed with sand from its bed and reached a semblance of clean. I purified water and drank deeply. Water bugs skidded around me. A small frog eyed me with suspicion. I fell asleep that night before the stars came out.

The next day I returned to that section of trail. I dug some more, and I dragged more fallen limbs. I gouged trenches and cross set logs to limit erosion. Using the multi tool, I hacked away invading vines. Sweat sketched through the dirt on my arms and legs to give me stripes. With a fallen tree for a lever, I pried and heaved a boulder into the brush. It was about two feet in diameter, and I considered at what mass did a rock become a boulder. When did it diminish enough to be just a stone? With enough size it could become a slab. Eroded enough it would be a pebble. I had read somewhere that Eskimos have over a hundred words for snow. There are many English words for rocks. They were piedras in Spanish and pierres in French and who knew what in German, Cantonese or Urdu. I wondered if there was a single, true name; something to call the platonic ideal of a rock. What significance would there be in knowing that name?

I became absorbed in repairing trail, and I gave it the same focus I used to apply to spreadsheets and financial statements. There was again a purpose. After pre-dawn coffee I hiked the couple miles with my makeshift shovel and multi-tool and started moving earth and rock and vegetable matter. I worked without a shirt in the cool autumn air, and each day my skin became the color of dirt. Kneeling and hunched over, I thought I might pass for one of the stones I worked to upturn. Hikers passed me and offered thanks or inquired about water and weather. I ignored them and focused on my tasks. I came to know rocks. There was purpose and need in my trail repair.

Things were forgotten in those days. The solar charger remained stuffed in the pack, and the cell phone lay dead in the tent. Some days I only ate whatever roots I happened to find in my excavation. Duncan's birthday came and went. Orion rose and fell unobserved. Once, digging away, I realized I had not put on my boots. Squatting nearly naked in the dirt, I smiled and kept at my work. Feet became yards, and yards became miles until I had reclaimed the trail back to my camp site. The labor was painful, but all pursuits carried costs, and I had narcotics.

I walked my section of trail clothed only in frayed shorts. I had not shaved in many days. I admired the tidy edge of flora, the smooth path, and the carefully inlaid erosion barriers. A youth group of hikers approached me. They announced their coming, long before I could see them, with their singing. When they emerged into view, all wearing blue t-shirts with "Jesus Rocks" emblazoned on the front, I stood to the side of the trail to let them pass.

"Do you like this section of trail?" I asked as they marched by. They were a clean scrubbed group and most had crosses dangling on their chests. They veered to the other side and walked on without making eye contact. Some of the girls giggled.

I wandered into the woods to look for mushrooms. I was not unaware. I just didn't care.

A few days later, I took a break from trail maintenance to resupply. I hiked the six or so miles to a town. At the outfitter, I purchased a new can of iso-pro fuel, a folding shovel and saw.

"How long you been out?" asked the guy in the shop.

"A few months," I replied. It was odd to hear my voice.

"You SoBo?"

"Yeah."

"You're on the home stretch man. Springer's only a few hundred miles."

I considered Springer Mountain; the end of the trail. I had not thought about that destination in some time. "I may or may not arrive at Springer Mountain, Georgia," I said early on. It seemed I was leaning toward "may not."

In Spellman's grocery store I bought packets of instant pasta, a log of hard salami, foil envelopes of tuna and salmon, coffee, and a bag of cashews. I picked up an onion, green pepper, zucchini, and broccoli. Since the produce didn't keep, resupply days were the only time for fresh vegetables other than those I foraged. I loaded all my groceries into a scale to check their weight. I guessed at four pounds, nine ounces as I loaded. It was four, eleven. In the butcher department, I stared at the cuts of red beef wrapped in plastic, and my mouth watered. It had been a long time since I'd had a nicely seasoned rib eye, medium rare. I lingered for a bit; wandering the aisles full of fantastic things.

I leaned against the stucco wall of the store and licked a cherry popsicle. It was a warm autumn afternoon, but the slight breeze carried hints of the change in cycle to come. The popsicle was cold.

Cold things were hard to come by on the trail.

I tried to remember the last time I had a drink with ice. When I was a boy, my mother would give my sisters and me change, and we would chase the ice cream truck down the street. The tinny circus music filled the neighborhood. My sisters bought creamsicles or drumsticks. I always got a popsicle.

A police car pulled up in front of me. It was an old Crown Victoria. The officer rolled down the passenger window and leaned across to look at me.

"Afternoon," he said with a southern drawl. He was young, perhaps mid twenties. His crisp uniform suggested pride in his work.

"Hello," I replied.

"I'm looking for a hiker."

"Well, you found one," I said. He laughed.

"A specific hiker. A guy named Finn. Trail name is Polar."

I paused in mid lick and stared at him.

I doubted the Internal Revenue Service or a collection agency would be searching the AT for me. I was still making child support payments from unemployment checks so Sarah probably wasn't after me again. I *had* assaulted that guy in the frozen food aisle. I didn't think any of the tribe would give up my name, and only Merlin knew me by anything other than Polar. I looked around the parking lot; reminded of the feeling I had in the psychiatrist's office when she said she was deciding whether to detain me.

"I think I saw that name in a few log books up North," I said. The melting popsicle dripped down my hand.

"Yeah. He's been missing since Harper's Ferry."

Recognition set in. I had not called the BSW in over two weeks. I was a missing person. I laughed at the irony, and the officer peered at me closely.

"Sorry. A lot of hikers choose to go missing," I said. He continued to study me. My hand was sticky with melted popsicle juice.

"What's your name?"

I thought for a second. "Nobody."

He gave me a blank look. He was waiting.

"That's my trail name," I said. "Nobody."

A plastic grocery sack blew across the parking lot. It drifted slowly, just above the ground.

"And your real name?" He put the cruiser into park and pulled out a notebook and a pen from a Comfort Inn. I thought about a good alias.

"Holden Caulfield," I said and hoped he wasn't a reader. I briefly wondered if it was a crime to lie to a police officer about one's identity.

He wrote the name in his notebook.

"Where you headed, Holden?"

"SoBo," I replied then added, "Southbound." He continued to stare at me. It occurred to me that he might ask for identification. I looked around again. There was a video store, a Pizza Hut and a nail salon. It was a long way back to the wood line.

"Your popsicle is melting."

I made a small lick that did nothing to slow the flow of cherry flavored sugar water.

"I should get back to eating it then."

There was a bit of irritation in his face.

"Well, have a good hike, Holden. If you run across Finn, aka Polar, please contact the authorities." He rolled up the window, done with me, and drove away.

I exhaled. The popsicle was dripping off my elbow and plopping on the ground. I licked up my forearm and headed back for the woods. Nothing to do but walk. The six mile hike back to the trail seemed much longer than it had been going into the town. You can't look over your shoulder while wearing a pack so I twisted my torso frequently to look back down the road behind me. Each sound of an approaching car caused an involuntary quickening of my pace. Finally, I saw the comforting white blaze on a tree and turned into the forest.

At my camp, I propped my bare feet on a log and looked up at the yellowing leaves. I felt strangely good about the deception of the police officer. It wasn't so much the success of it but rather a feeling of shedding again. Much as I had discarded weight from my pack and my body, my shorts then only staying up because of a tightened belt, it seemed I had shed yet another version of me. Polar was a man with honor and standing in a tribe.

Nobody was alone in the woods with only the trail and the trees, and he was happy with that.

. . .

The next day I went to work on a new section of trail. The work was easier with the shovel and saw. Digging through seasons of leaves I came upon a snake skin. I wondered where the snake was and how many more skins it had abandoned. The metaphor was not lost on me. I held up the skin, and the sunlight glowed through it.

"Where are you, snake?" I asked. It did not respond.

"Can you escape by shedding?" I asked again. There was still no response, and I tore the skin into small pieces. It flaked like parchment.

Athlete, son, trophy, professional, husband, father, provider, dependent, even member of society...I had lost many skins. Some I shed; others were ripped from my hide. I continued to dig. I enjoyed the clean smells of dirt and natural decay. Nobody did not need a skin. A grasshopper, woozy in the cool autumn air, crashed near me. I speared it with my knife. As it jerked, I pulled off the legs and head and popped the body into my mouth. It crunched as I chewed, and its bitter protein touched my tongue. I went back to digging.

...

We lay naked in bed. The blankets were pulled up against a frigid New England winter night. I could hear the wind screaming and the faint crash of the waves. I traced circles with my fingertips on the small of her back. She stretched like a cat and looked at me.

"You are my beautiful, sunny woman."

She arched her back against my touch and smiled.

"I love you," she said.

"Yeah, but I love you *so much*."

The dogs, banished from the room during the act, leaped on the bed. Bailey did his best to curl into a ball and go unnoticed.

"You're not small," she said and laughed.

I watched her. She scratched Bailey's ears, and he sprawled out. Her eyes, hooded and reserved with most people, always shined with animals and often with me.

"I want eggs," she announced. She threw back the blankets, rose, and pulled on my hooded sweatshirt. It hung to her thighs, and she looked more beautiful in it than the satin nightgown she had worn to bed.

We cooked eggs with shallots and garlic and topped them with a quick salsa of tomatoes, onion and pickled jalapenos. We wrapped a blanket around us and ate as we looked out at the horizontal snow and the ocean crashing against the sea wall. The dogs hovered hoping for a dropped morsel. I reached out and brushed her hair behind her ear. She ducked, she didn't like that, but she smiled at me. I looked long into her eyes. She had told me they were green but sometimes brown. I couldn't tell.

"I love you so much."

I was happy in my shack by the sea. I was happy with my BSW.

I lost count of days. I dug. I sawed. I repaired. I worked south, hiking a few miles each day and then working on trail. By the falling leaves I guessed it was October, but I wasn't sure in the foreign southern land. Fewer SoBo's were passing by, thanking me for my work. When they would approach, I would rise with shovel in one hand and saw in the other. I nodded at them. They hurried along, and I went back to work.

Back at my camp I found a possum in the trap. I had woven a basket from vines. It was propped up with a stick over a piece of salami. A rock on top of the basket weighed it down. The possum had taken the bait and was hissing in the cage.

I calmly bashed its head with a log.

When it was done writhing I skinned it. I slit it from asshole to chin, pulling the hide away from the pale flesh, and stuck it on a spit over the fire. I wiped my bloody hands on my shorts and sat down.

With enough hot sauce and hunger, most things are edible. I gnawed the charred meat and looked at the cell phone. I had pulled it out of the pack that morning. It was dead, but I could bring it to life with the solar charger. I owed her so much but at least a call. I watched the stars wheel above the almost naked trees until Orion appeared. I looked at the three stars of the belt with detachment. The phone was up to three bars of power, and I turned it on.

There were one hundred and twelve missed calls and nineteen voice mails. I assumed the mailbox was full. The missed calls followed a bell curve. There were a few in the days since I let the phone die. They increased in the following weeks to nearly twenty on one day then dwindled. The last was three days ago. Nearly all were from the BSW. The last asked, "Are you fucking dead?" Some were from Frog. A couple of them were from collection agencies. One was from a headhunter offering me a job. None were from Shane or Quinn. I saw that the date was October thirty first. Trick or treat.

I laughed and added wood to the fire. Orion looked down.

"Fuck you," I said looking up at him and ripped a chunk of meat from the possum thigh and held it with greasy fingers with swollen knuckles. I still had seventy two Percocet and another month's worth of prednisone. I could get my rheumatologist to keep refilling the prednisone scripts, but they wouldn't keep me going. I put the Percocet and the quarter bottle of rum back in the pack. Nobody didn't need them yet.

I called her, and the phone rang until it went to voicemail. "I'm alive," I said and hung up. I turned off the phone. I didn't want her return call. Perhaps some part of me, some remaining skin of Finn, was afraid there wouldn't be one, and mine was preemptive.

I chewed on a rib bone and glared up at Orion grinning down at me. He laughed at me, and I threw the bone at the sky.

. . .

Waking in the early dawn, I shivered, wrapped the sleeping bag over my shoulders and got up to stir the embers of the fire. I added some wood and blew until it caught flame. With the perpetual fresh start that new days always force upon us, I was more Polar than Nobody, more Finn than Polar. I evolved in the rhythm of a spinning earth and then reset. The journal was open, and the photos were on the ground. I looked at the phone and considered calling again. A photo of Keegan leaping off a sand dune caught my eye. He was seventeen in the picture. He'd just graduated from high school. We'd talked that day about his plans for college, that he wanted to start a band, and he wanted to backpack across Europe. He had big dreams.

I pulled plastic bags from the pack. One contained a pile of cowshit. The other had strands of morning glory I had found. The blue flowers were withered. I cut the mushrooms from the shit, washed them and dumped them in the pot. I plucked the seeds from the morning glory, ground them between rocks and added them in. For good measure, I dropped in a Percocet and brought it all to a boil. I hadn't tried that before, and I didn't know what the effect would be. I just wanted to see my son.

The concoction tasted like shit and didn't seem to do much except make me drowsy. I sat by the fire and drew circles in the dirt with my finger. The circles became a constellation, Orion brought to earth. The dirt stars seemed to flicker and shine.

In the dim flicker I saw Keegan sitting across from me. I looked away then back, and he was still there. He still had the shaggy brown hair and a hairline that had begun retreating early and the wispy, half assed goatee he could never get to fill in. His eyes still gleamed like he always knew something you didn't. He did not have the massive dent in his skull I had seen the last time I looked at him in the morgue. I leaned toward him.

"Hey, Pop," he said. I remembered that voice and all its variations from the squeak of a little boy to the cracking teen to the soft but deep voice of the young man he grew to be. It was a voice that suggested that just about everything was funny, and the listener just had to figure out what it was.

"Keeg?"

He looked up at the remains of the possum carcass I had strung up a tree.

"That's gross, Dad."

Tears filled my eyes and dripped down my cheeks.

"I miss you so much," I said. The flames flickered, and he was gone. The dirt stars faded to dark spots. I brushed them out of existence with my hand and sat remembering every detail of his face and the sound of his voice. Perhaps I slept. I wasn't sure.

I wiped away the tears, kicked some dirt on the fire, picked up my shovel and saw, and set off through the gloom. The world was shades of grey in the early dawn. Dark skeletons of trees reached up toward an ashen sky. In places, mist clung to the ground. The only sound was that of my own footsteps on desiccated, grey leaves. I crossed a sluggish stream that looked inky black. Perhaps it was the Styx.

Keegan visited me more; always at night and never for very long. Each time he faded away like mist in sunlight. I experimented with different amounts of mushrooms, seeds and narcotics trying to make his visits last longer. I was rational enough to know I was hallucinating, but seeing my son again seemed a fair trade for whatever I was doing to my sanity.

"What are you doing out here, Dad?" he asked.

"Fixing trail."

"You know what I mean."

I poked at the fire with a stick and looked up to his face.

"Just walking."

"Do you remember fun, Dad?" I was hallucinating conversations with my dead son, and my mind had decided to make him Jiminy fucking Cricket.

"Remember when we made the water balloon launcher with surgical tubing and blew out Mrs. Carson's window?" he asked. "Mom was pissed!"

I laughed at the memory.

"I remember everything we did, Keegan," I said softly, looking down and digging at the dirt with my heel.

"Have some fun again, Dad. Shane and Quinn need you." His eyes gleamed in the firelight. I reached across to touch him, wanting so much to tousle that hair as I had done thousands of times. He faded away, as he always did, before my hand could reach him. My hand was extended, reaching out to nothing, and the fire burned the hairs on my arm.

The darkness pressed in close to me as if a physical presence. It seemed the fire could not repel it. That song popped into my head:

Darkness comes
And I'm goin' home

I wondered abstractly what Dr. Frankenfucker or the Transylvanian psychiatrist would make of this. It seemed I was pushing into new ground beyond the depression, suicidal tendencies and bipolar disorder. At least I was still overachieving in one facet. I laughed in the dark. I was curious whether awareness of mental instability was a good or bad indicator. I had learned long ago that one descent was always followed by another. There was always another stairwell leading down, and the upper floor was always better by comparison. So, I didn't worry too much. Worse shit would come. At least in that circle of hell I got to see Keegan.

A twig snapped in the darkness. I peered out, and the yellow eyes of a coyote looked back at me. He slinked forward to the edge of my small circle of light; eyeing the possum carcass that was still dangling above. I could see the outline of ribs on his shadowy frame and thought he was in deep shit for the coming winter.

"Find your own food," I said.

"Huntin's been tough, and I was chased away from the dumpster," I decided he would say, and he would speak with a southern accent. I laughed.

"What's funny?" he asked.

"Nothing." I rose, cut down the carcass and tossed it to him. He sniffed at it and turned it over with a paw. Then, he lifted it in his mouth.

"Much obliged," he mumbled through a mouth full of possum remnants and vanished into the dark.

I considered if I had imagined him or if he was real. It didn't matter. He wasn't Keegan. I crawled in the tent and slept and dreamed of a pack of wolves attacking a deer. Some of them spoke Russian, and I could not understand what they were saying. I alternated being a wolf and being the deer. I tasted the blood when I sunk my fangs into the hindquarter, and I felt the pain of having my flesh ripped.

• • •

I hiked long and hard the next day along the spine of the Shenandoah ridge. The trail was well maintained there, and I could find nothing to repair. Cresting a hill I would find a long stretch of wide, smooth trail. I swore and walked faster. Each turn and crest revealed the same thing.

When night descended, I pitched my tent a few yards off the trail and went to sleep angry and frustrated.

The next day was the same, and the one after that. I came upon a freshly sawn deadfall near the trail and yelled "Fuck," into the forest. I hiked a hundred miles and could not find a fucking thing to fix. In four days I did not see another person; although I occasionally heard a laugh or bit of conversation on the wind. I found it odd since the AT in Virginia is among the highest trafficked sections.

I threw the shovel into the forest. The last bit of purpose was gone. Since there were no people, I pitched my tent in the middle of the trail. I made my special tea, and I dreamed of being buffeted by storms and gods hurling curses.

• • •

I awoke in the spring. At least, it seemed to be spring, and I wondered if I'd slept right through winter. The trees were adorned with fresh green leaves. Tulips were peeking through the forest floor. A mother raccoon and her two babies bounced past me. The air was fresh like laundry washed with Gain detergent. I found tender roots of early season turnips and ate them straight from the ground.

Wandering through the reborn forest, I was reminded of the awesome beauty and force of nature. Rebirth and regeneration were happening all around me. A butterfly, maybe a buttercup, struggled from its cocoon.

A blue flower burst through a remnant of snow in a shady spot. My bare feet became numb on ground that still carried winter's chill.

I joined a family of lizards on a slab of rock and enjoyed its reflective warmth. The sun, still on a soft angle, made promises of the heat it would bring. Overhead, a young sparrow left the nest. It flapped mightily and careened through the air before coming to rest on a lower branch; first flight success.

I watched the magic about me and wondered if I was dead. Flowers sprouted and blossomed in front of me. Perhaps I had learned to hibernate, and I was dreaming away the dark and bitter winter. My fingers were straight and thin. My wrists could bend, and I rolled over to do pushups because I could. I laughed, and the lizards laughed with me.

Down the hill I found a stream. It flowed clear and cold with winter's melted runoff. I put my face to the surface and drank deeply until the cold water burned my chest. Trout gleamed beneath. Their bright hues shone as they darted about.

I wandered about the forest marveling at each new sight, sound and smell. A neon cloud of dragonflies buzzed about me with an electric hum then sped off with dragonfly purpose. Wild coriander burst in a meadow with the scent of burnt butter. A towering oak tree sprouted millions of leaves. I ran with a doe and her fawn, leaping over logs and across creeks. The dappled young one paused occasionally to let me catch up.

Back at my tent, I noticed there was no trail. The only indication of human existence was me. I turned on the cell phone, but it had no signal. The needle on the compass just spun back and forth; unable to find true north, or even a false north. I leaned against a mossy log and ate raspberries that bloomed and ripened in front of me.

By late afternoon, it was autumn. Leaves turned vivid shades of orange and red. Squirrels busied themselves stockpiling acorns. The air was crisp and cool. A black bear meandered past, fattened and with a thick coat. I fell asleep as the first heavy snowflakes of winter fell.

I awoke and lay in the sleeping bag looking at the walls of the tent. A spider was spinning a web above me. I unzipped the door and peered out. The Eden or hell or hallucination or whatever it might have been was gone. It was a grey and dreary day with cold rain spitting down. Looking left then right, I could see the trail extending away.

I cooked oatmeal and made regular tea not because I was hungry but just because that's what I always did on cold mornings. Wrapped and hooded in my rain jacket, I broke down my camp and packed up. I pulled the green rain cover over the pack and tightened it to my back. With it against the brown jacket, I imagined I looked like a large, ambulatory mushroom. Nothing to do but walk.

I trudged along in the wet, grey world and thought about the spectacle of the place I had been before.

In the afternoon, I passed my father. He was hiking the other direction. He said nothing and did not look at me as he passed. I stopped and turned.

"Dad?"

He looked back with a scowl and kept walking.

Later, Sellers hiked by. He still had the gunshot wound in his temple, and much of his head was missing. He did not say anything either. The parade of ghosts, some living and some dead, continued through the day. I saw my grandmother in her blue housecoat and slippers with her yappy little dog that she would put in a high chair to eat at the kitchen table. She gave me a look of disdain. She had never liked me, and I had hated her. My high school wrestling coach went by. While I was resting on a rock to the side of the trail, half my old platoon passed. They were spread out in patrol formation, their faces were painted in camouflage, and their M-16's were held at the ready. The acrid smell of gunpowder passed with them.

"Reilly?" I called as he passed. He looked at me, pulled his index finger from the trigger and held it to his lips then crept away into the wood line. On my birthday one year, Reilly and I stayed up all night drinking PBR's then drove a Bradley into a river the next morning.

A line of old girlfriends went by. There was Julie. I went to the prom with her. Shawna, whom I lost my virginity to in my second week of college, walked past. In the middle of the group was Sarah. She looked pissed off as usual. The BSW was not among the group.

I continued to hike and wondered if I would be visited by the ghost of Christmas future. That made me laugh. Heidi, the German Shepherd I had when I was a little boy, ran through the woods chasing Ming, my sister's old cat.

So, I was definitely off the rails. It didn't seem so bad. So I saw a few dead people and others who had passed in and out of my life? I could consciously torture myself better than my subconscious was doing so far.

Hubris has been the downfall of many heroes.

At the end of a long, damp, grey day, I made camp beneath a spreading pine. I started a fire with its fallen needles and fed it with pine cones. The smell of the pine smoke wafted on the air, and I added bigger fuel until the flames were leaping toward the sky. I cooked fettuccine and added a packet of tuna for protein and Tabasco for a little flavor. It seemed the rational thing to do. Eating from the pot, I watched the gloom of dusk descend on the forest around me.

I heard footsteps in the dry pine needles and waited, curious to see who might pass by next. First came Keegan. He was wearing the same Guinness t-shirt and slouchy jeans I had seen him in before. He smiled at me, but it seemed a sad smile, one of pity. Next came Shane. She still had the plump cheeks and freckles she had never outgrown. She waddled past holding her very pregnant belly. I looked at her left hand. There was a big wedding ring. Duncan followed. He had grown in the couple years since I had seen him. His faux hawk had been replaced with stringy, greasy hair. He was taller than I would have expected and lanky. There were dark bruise marks on his arms. Then came Quinn. She was still small and cute. It was her eyes that were different. The bright, curious eyes I knew were dark and downcast. She was the only one who did not look at me. Her gaze remained firmly on the ground. Last came the BSW. Her hair was longer, and the look she gave me was one of indifference. She glanced at me as if appraising then looked away into the forest.

I rose and rushed after them. I reached for Quinn, wanting to hold her tight. She evaporated as I reached her. I ran around the forest trying to reach one of them; to touch and hold them. Each faded away at my approach. In the growing darkness I could hear Duncan laughing then that too drifted away.

I returned to the fire and slumped down. I had to give my mind credit. That was pretty fucking clever. I tried to recall each of them and how they just looked, but even those memories darted away. I would be denied even that. Well played, mind. Even as I reached for memories, they were erased. I could no longer see Shane in her homecoming dress or Quinn on her first day of school or the BSW the first time I said, "I love you."

The scream I heard was my own. It took me a moment to realize that. It was a guttural, wild noise; one an animal might make. I rose and walked into the dark. Perhaps I could still find them. I thrashed about. Branches caught and cut my face. I fell into a gully and lay in the cold mud and decaying leaves. The smell of rot was all around me. I called out to Keegan then Quinn then Duncan and then Shane. There was no answer. Finally, I called for the BSW. She always came.

"Penny," I yelled, then again louder and louder.

My cries echoed in the woods and silence returned. I had no strength to rise so I lay there and shivered in the night until sleep kindly came. My dreams were troubled, and I had difficulty distinguishing between the sleeping dreams and the waking ones. Quinn miscarried the baby I had seen her carrying. She cried in a hospital bed and a tiny bundle was carried away by a nurse as she looked on with longing.

When dawn was a whisper in the sky, I rose and made my way back to camp. The world was a scale of grey. The dark, hulking outlines of trees loomed above in contrast to the lightening sky. It looked like a film negative. It was stark and simple without the clutter of color.

Wrapped in my sleeping bag, I collected wood. I whittled away at a stick until there were enough shavings to light. They curled and shrank at the touch of the match, and I fed first twigs then sticks and finally a log. The licking flames brought color back to the world. I huddled close and felt the heat begin returning to my bones.

"Well, Finn, you're in the middle of fucking nowhere and losing your mind," I said out loud. The sound of the words seemed to crack through the stillness of the dawn. Somewhere above, there was a beating of wings, and a bird took flight.

"All things considered, I guess it's better to be crazy in the woods than crazy in a hospital." The sound of my voice was somehow comforting. I thought about the hospital ward with the off white walls and doors that locked from the other side. The forest was definitely better.

I watched the world beyond the firelight's reach take on form and color in preparation for the sun's arrival. It seemed a rather extravagant entrance for a routine and daily event. The sunlight reached the tops of the trees first. They glowed while below was still steeped in grey - like ashes.

I added logs to make a white man fire. My grandfather used to say Indians, it was before they became Native Americans, built small fires and stood close, and white men built big fires and stood way back. The heat radiated in the morning air. The smoke drifted up to the sunlight and remained grey. The sun had no power to give it color.

"Are you hungry?" I asked a chipmunk who had come to investigate me. Maybe he too wanted some warmth. I tore open a granola bar and tossed chunks to him. When his cheeks were bulging, he scampered up a tree. The sun reached my feet first, and I watched the line of light travel up my body until it dazzled against my face.

My eyelids were heavy. There had been little rest in the woods that night. I took two Percocet. Not because I was in pain but because I wanted to cloud my betraying mind and sleep without dreams.

Part 3

The office was warm and comfortable. The walls, sort of a sandstone red, were lined with pictures of waterfalls and sunsets and several framed diplomas. A vanilla-scented candle burned on a shelf. There was an overstuffed chair, a small table and a couch. I thought it was funny that there was actually a couch. Dr. Smith was a middle-aged guy with thinning blonde hair and round, wire-rimmed glasses. He wore a light blue shirt, paisley tie, khaki slacks and running shoes.

"Hi, I'm John," he said and extended his hand.

"Finn."

He gestured toward the couch, and I sat. I wondered if I was supposed to lie down.

"So, what brings you here?" he asked.

"I'm having panic attacks, and I can't sleep." I looked at a picture on the wall of a waterfall cascading down a slot canyon. I recognized it. It was in Zion National Park. I had hiked that canyon. Had John hiked it?

He asked me lots of questions about my pending divorce, my relationship with Sarah, my children, my parents, my job, my mood, my emotions, and my sex life. As I answered, he wrote continuously with a pencil on a yellow legal pad. I recognized another picture on the wall as the Grand Teton. Sellers and I had climbed that. A small clock on a shelf ticked. It felt like a job interview.

"I believe you are suffering from depression and bipolar disorder," he announced.

"Excellent." I glanced at my watch. He had deduced that in just over a half hour.

He went on to recommend a combination of medications and therapy. He practiced cognitive therapy which sought to change my perceptions and thus change my behavior. I looked at another picture of an alpine waterfall. I could not place its location.

That was my first time on the couch. There would be other couches in equally comfortable offices. I left with prescriptions for antipsychotics, mood stabilizers, and antidepressants. I visited John twice a week at one hundred fifty bucks a pop. Seroquel, the antipsychotic made me feel like a zombie, without feeling or emotion, and I was okay with that. I didn't want to feel.

"Do you miss your children?" he asked me once.

"Yes."

"Tell me more about that."

"I miss them…a lot."

John was big on "doing the work" as he called it. I really didn't know what that meant. He asked questions. I answered. I kept waiting for a breakthrough or even some incremental improvement. Instead, I popped pills that removed my emotions. Two days after the last time I saw John, I tried to kill myself. He billed me for the appointment I missed while I was locked in the nuthouse.

...

The skunk was fat, ready for winter. He was intently clawing at a pile of soggy leaves, and I was curious what prize was in there. The two white stripes on his back undulated as he worked. I was downwind from him and could smell him. The odor was a combination of sulfur and burnt rubber. Still, being downwind meant he couldn't smell me. I remained perched on my rock and watched. Skunks are solitary animals. They are shunned by the other citizens of the forest and don't even hang out with other skunks. I wondered if they found the smell of other skunks to be repulsive in the same way that the other animals and I did.

"Dude, you fucking smell!" I imagined one skunk exclaiming to another.

The skunk pulled a lizard from the leaves. It appeared to be already dead and hung limply in the skunk's mouth. He lifted his nose to the air, testing the environment, and waddled into the brush with his breakfast.

I leaned back against the cold granite. I could see a white blaze on a tree in the distance. The weak morning sun had not instilled any heat into the rock yet. In the afternoon, lizards would lounge on it and enjoy the warmth. Perhaps they would hold a vigil for their dead friend. With one eye always spinning toward the sky to watch for birds, the other eye might cast down in sorrow for the loved one lost. Perhaps an elder lizard, a grizzled survivor of bird and skunk attacks, might say a few words. In the midst of his eulogy, his tongue would lash out to suck in a fly that wandered too close. Then, somewhere else in the forest, the flies would buzz their grief. Death was constant and pervasive. The fecundity of the world seemed only to serve in replenishing the buffet of death. Everywhere, different rungs of the food chain were in mourning. Except the lonely skunk, his neck maybe snapped in the jaws of a coyote, would not be mourned or missed. I would mourn the skunk.

The world seemed concrete and conventional as I sat there pondering skunk memorial services. Birds chirped. Dry leaves rustled in the breeze. The rock was solid beneath me. A few lazy clouds drifted above. There was no indication that my mind was fucking with me at the moment. I considered that it would be really clever of my mind to hallucinate a mundane moment such as that. Perhaps I was really in my tent, shivering in my sleeping bag. Perhaps I was strapped to a bed in a hospital somewhere with an intravenous line dripping some chemical cocktail into me. It was odd to distrust one's own thoughts. It seemed like the ultimate of betrayals. Still, if I were in a hospital, having me believe I was sitting quietly in the forest thinking about skunk funerals would be a kindness. I wondered where Kurtz thought he was while he sweated in his jungle cave.

I didn't feel crazy, although I wasn't sure just how crazy was supposed to feel. I had known manic episodes when I had stayed awake for almost three days and lost over six thousand dollars playing online poker. I had known panic attacks when my hands went numb, my vision blurred into a tunnel, and my heart pulsed as if ready to burst through my ribcage. I had known depression so deep I couldn't muster the effort to even try killing myself. All those had occurred while I was reassured by trained professionals that I was quite sane.

A grasshopper bounced onto my leg and paused to survey things with his bulging eyes then careened away. I wondered if grasshoppers had mental illness.

"Fred, you are not a yeti! You're a grasshopper!" The therapist grasshopper might tell his patient.

Maybe the hallucinations had been just an "episode" as they used to call any behavior that could not be explained. Perhaps, without my hallucinogenic concoction, my brain had returned to its regularly scheduled program. In the absence of any other information, I had to assume I really was just sitting on a rock in the woods thinking about skunk deaths and psychotic grasshoppers. The obvious fear was when the next episode would come. Many doctors had told me that mental illness, such as depression, was a real infirmity, and that I couldn't just "get better". It required real medications. I always asked, if that was the case, what the point of therapy was. They never liked that question.

A couple hikers came along the trail. From my rock, I saw them a couple hundred yards out. I watched as they made their way toward me. They prodded the ground with their hiking poles and moved at a good pace. He was tall and wore a North Face beanie. She had a teddy bear tied to her pack. I was only a few yards off the trail, but I hoped they might pass by without conversation.

"Morning," he said and paused to sip water. She unbuckled her pack. I sighed.

"Morning."

"Good day for a hike," she said. I tried to think of the last time I had seen a person; a real person. I assumed they were real. She was probably in her early thirties, and her blonde hair was braided into pigtails.

"How long you been out?" he asked. He had a gold hoop in his left ear.

"A few months," I replied, then after a few seconds, added, "How about you?"

"Wow," she said. He fished a Ziploc bag of gorp out of his pack, took a handful and passed it to her. She took a few bites and offered it to me.

"No thank you."

"We're out for seven days. Trying to get a hundred mile section done," he said.

I watched a passing cloud and wondered if skunks preferred burial or cremation.

"Are you SoBo?" she asked.

"Yes."

"We're doing it in sections. After this one, we'll have almost half the trail completed," he said.

The cloud passed behind the treetops.

"Are you going all the way to Springer?" she asked.

I watched a line of ants hauling away pieces of a dead caterpillar on the rock. They were black and medium-sized as far as ants go. I didn't know much about ants. The red ones stung. They seemed to come in a variety of sizes. They were always busy. Ignorance of ants did not bother me as ignorance of butterflies had. They would continue their industry regardless of my knowledge.

"Maybe."

He lifted her pack and helped her put it on. She fastened the buckles. He pulled on the straps of his own pack.

"Well, have a good hike," she said. He had already started down the trail.

"You too." She walked away, and the teddy bear bounced with her strides.

Having not had a conversation in quite a while, I thought it had gone pretty well. I leaned my head back against the rock. It was a little warmer than it had been earlier. A squirrel came to examine the crumbs of food they had dropped. He leaned back on his bushy tail and nibbled at a peanut. Squirrels were social animals. They probably had big, lavish funeral services with lots of lamenting. Chipmunks and rabbits were probably invited.

The forest had its normal level of sound. There was mostly silence occasionally interrupted by something scampering in the brush, the call of a bird, or the rattle of dry leaves still clinging to their hosts. The morning was turning into a beautiful, Indian summer day. It was the kind of day when families might pick apples or walk through a pumpkin patch. I sat on my rock, closed my eyes, and listened to myself breathe. The breaths were deep and slow.

For the first time since I had aimed south and started walking, I thought about turning around. It would be colder hiking north though. I had been in the wilderness for months. I still didn't know what I was hiking toward. It was evident that my mind was not going to leave behind anything I might be hiking away from. I remained a meanderer. It took Odysseus ten years to get home. Moses spent forty years wandering in the desert. Was returning inexorable? Returning is what heroes did.

I opened my eyes. A young buck was in the glade. His small spikes were losing their velvet, and it hung in tatters. He peered about nervously between bites of grass. Occasionally he would freeze, listening to some sound his deer ears detected and my human ones could not. I remained still with my breathing slow and quiet. I would do my best not to interrupt his brunch. He wandered about the meadow pausing to sample a leaf or clump of grass that looked more enticing than others. He ate. I watched.

Was returning to the world required? Things were safer and simpler in the wilderness. Bad news did not travel through trees. Stay alert and cautious like the buck. Work for food like the ants. Rejoice in the treat of a dead lizard like the skunk. Perhaps the skunk would mourn me. Maybe the squirrels and chipmunks I had shared so many meals with would come to my services and lament, if nothing else, a source of tasty granola. I would provide a feast for the coyotes and crows.

I coughed. The deer's head jerked up. For an instant, he froze and stared at me. Then, he bounded, and in a couple leaps was gone into the forest. As much as I felt so, as much as I tried, I couldn't really be part of that world.

There were responsibilities: child support, alimony, back taxes. Quinn needed braces. Outside of putting a signature on a check, I didn't know if my absence from the world was good or bad. Was the BSW better off with me wandering in the woods? Perhaps I was less the hero of the story and more the Cyclops who lived as a hermit in the wilderness to protect others from himself. I did miss her. I missed my children. Yet, they were all part of a world I was not ready to face again. I was without a home.

· · ·

The covered bridge was a long white tunnel, and my footsteps echoed as I passed through. It reminded me of the bridges in New England and seemed a little odd. I didn't know they had covered bridges in the south. I walked into Mintaka, Tennessee. I had not known where I was until I saw the sign welcoming me. Digging and hallucinating, I had hiked five hundred miles of Virginia and barely noticed. The downtown was lined with squat brick buildings. They had once been banks and department stores. Now they were gift shops, galleries, coffee houses and bars. The place had given itself to tourism. At least the buildings weren't boarded up.

I found an ATM and got cash. It took me a moment to remember the PIN. My balance was still pretty good. Meandering in the wilderness was certainly an economical way to live. A minivan with Ohio license plates passed by, and the children inside stared at me. They were all redheaded and with freckles. If the early stages of the journey had been a tourist visa to the trail, and the middle parts dual citizenship, I was now a foreigner visiting this world and still not fully part of the other. I wandered along the main street looking in windows. One display had intricately carved wooden statues of bears, wolves, owls and such. I wondered how much they weighed.

There was a library a few buildings up and a block off the main street. It had brightly painted walls but still was filled with the musty smell of books. The old woman behind the counter inspected me over the top of the glasses perched at the end of her nose.

"Please leave your backpack and stick outside," she said with a heavy southern drawl. I went outside and dropped my pack and stick.

"There is a fifteen minute limit for computer use," she called out behind me as I sat down. I looked at the teenage boy at the other computer and the nearly empty, extra large soda cup beside him.

The keys on the keyboard were smooth. The desktop wallpaper, a picture of the covered bridge I had walked through, seemed very bright. I let my hands sit on the keyboard. My fingers went naturally to the home row keys, and I could feel the small bumps on the F and J keys. I slid the mouse and opened a browser. The pictures and links and headlines that popped up were jarring. I breathed in, held it, and opened my email. There were hundreds of unread emails. I deleted all those announcing sales, telling me sports scores or selling me Viagra. Then, I stared at the unopened ones that remained. Some were from the BSW. A few were from Sarah. Frog had sent a few. A couple were from my mother. One was from my sister.

I breathed in again. Sarah wanted to know where the fuck I was and why I had not called my daughter in two months. My mother told me about her trip to Yellowstone, she saw deer and elk but no bears, and hoped I was enjoying my walk.

I sent an email to Shane and Quinn with a few pictures I had taken along the way and told them I loved them very much.

"I love you. I miss you. I'm so worried. Please come home," was the last email from the BSW. It was from a few days prior.

"I love you. I'm okay. I'm still walking," I replied. I knew it wasn't adequate, but I didn't know what else to say. Whether my actions were defined as selfish or self-protecting or something between, I still did not want to be cruel. I wasn't sure if her knowing I was okay and still wandering was kindness or cruelty. I hoped it to be the former.

I wasn't even going to open my sister's email. I didn't really care to hear about her fabulous trip to Scottsdale or the new thoroughbred horse she had, or whatever it was going to be. There was no subject header for the email so I clicked on it.

Our father had died three weeks earlier. He had a massive heart attack in the home he shared with his girlfriend in Mexico. Per his request, he was buried down there.

I closed the browser and sat there. The teenage boy sucked the last of his soda. There was the sound of a fly buzzing somewhere in the room above the faint hum of the computers. I had not spoken to my father in over four years. I tried to remember our last conversation. I knew it was a fight but couldn't remember what it was about.

"Your time is up," the old woman announced.

I rose and paused at a table of books for sale. I picked up a paperback collection of American drama that included *Long Day's Journey into Night* and *Death of a Salesman*. I thought that was kind of funny.

"How much?" I asked.

"They're free for hikers," the old woman said with a degree of disgust.

Outside, a crisp autumn breeze blew and carried the scent of burning leaves. I lifted my pack and stood looking at the houses with tidy yards, picket fences and two car garages.

Bad news doesn't travel through trees.

• • •

The grocery store was not the normally dazzling experience. I moved quickly through the aisles collecting instant pasta, oatmeal, foil envelopes of tuna and salmon, a ginger root, a clove of garlic and granola bars. I did pick up a couple chocolate bars. Next door was a liquor store, and I bought a pint of Southern Comfort.

A police car cruised slowly by me as I walked along the sidewalk. A mother approaching me ushered her children to the side as I passed. A man with a camouflage baseball cap in a pickup truck stared at me at a red light. The truck was blue with a primer grey right front quarter panel. I quickened my pace to the outfitter down the road. The rules of the wilderness were simple, but they were absolute: water, food, warmth.

I could not leave until they were fulfilled.

A bell rang on the outfitter's door when I opened it, and I was greeted by the smell of ski wax. It was warm and crowded with merchandise inside, and it reminded me of Three Miles' shop far to the north.

"Howdy," a man folding sweaters called out to me. His hair was pulled into a long brown ponytail. I nodded. Outfitters were like embassies for hikers in hostile towns.

"I hope you're SoBo," he said. "The weather's turning."

"I am." I picked up a fuel canister, waterproof matches, and water purifying drops.

"There's hot coffee over there."

"Thanks." I found a black fleece jacket, a wool hat and gloves.

"I'm Ice," he said. I poured a cup of coffee and looked at the bulletin board hanging on the wall. There was a handwritten note pinned to it that said "Polar, call Frog."

"I'm…" and I paused, "Nobody." He laughed.

"Like Odysseus?"

"Yeah, sort of." The coffee was cheap quality, maybe Folger's, and old and smelled a little like turpentine. He went into a backroom, and I pulled the note down. I wrote, "Frog, I'm okay. Polar" then pinned it back up. The pine cone telegraph would get the message through.

"Take a load off," he said when he returned and gestured toward a chair near a fireplace.

"I still have some miles to put in today," and I put my items on the counter to ring up.

"Have a good hike, Nobody."

I pulled on the jacket and shoved the rest into my pack. The wind had picked up, dark clouds were rolling over the hilltops, and I walked quickly back through the town with my head down. The police car cruised past me again. I paused outside a pub. They probably called it a bar in that part of the world. Laughter and the sounds of a football game came from inside. I looked up at the officers in the passing police car, held their gaze, pulled off my pack, and walked in. I set the pack and stick near the door.

Inside was dim, except for televisions and a lighted Jaegermeister display. Smoke hung heavy and acrid in the air. I had forgotten there were still places where you could smoke indoors. There were just a few people inside, but all eyes turned toward me. An old man with a fat belly and overalls looked at me and then ignored me. A young couple, him with a hunter orange sweatshirt and her with a too small shirt that said "princess," glanced at me and went back to their conversation. The bartender, middle-aged and probably pretty at some point in her past, put down her cigarette.

"You have money?" she asked.

"May I have a Sam Adams?" I put a twenty on the bar.

"We ain't got that."

"How about a Heineken?" I looked at the limited selection of liquors on the shelf. "And a shot of Wild Turkey." I wasn't much of a whiskey connoisseur but, even at my most suicidal moments, I wouldn't drink shitty beer.

"You're a good daddy," the woman in the princess shirt said to her boyfriend.

"She wants sixty five bucks a week. How much does a baby cost?" he said.

The bartender put the drinks in front of me and took the twenty. I drank the shot, feeling the heat slide down my torso, and sipped the beer. It was cold and tasted good. The couple asked to settle up.

"We gotta get home to the puppy. She's in her first heat," the woman said.

"Before the other one decides to fuck her," he added.

The bartender told them about a vet outside of town who would "fix a bitch" for a hundred twenty five bucks.

"Shit. That ain't even one good night of drinkin' money for us," the guy said. His girlfriend laughed.

"That's almost double sixty five," I said. I finished the beer, picked up my change, leaving a hundred percent tip to maybe help the next hiker who entered the place, and walked out while they were still doing math and trying to determine if they'd been insulted. I briefly considered staying for a good bar fight, but discretion won out. My father wasn't around to bail me out of jail any more.

The covered bridge loomed empty, like a tunnel between worlds. The wind whistled inside it. On the other side, I found a white blaze on a tree and turned back into the wood line.

Back among the trees, my pace slowed. I realized I was panting. A wide log with moss growing on it lay to the right. I clambered through the undergrowth to it and, on its dark northern side, found mushrooms. I harvested them with my knife and deposited them into the side pocket of the pack.

I hiked slowly back up toward the ridge. I was watching the ground and stopped often to examine leaves or wander off trail to investigate a plant that caught my eye. In a glade that was dappled with sun just before the clouds covered it, I found Indian turnip. It was poisonous raw but delicious when cooked. Further along, I found a wild mustard plant. Dinner would be good.

Just off the ridgeline on the leeward side, next to a sheltering boulder and beneath the wide spread of a fir tree, I pitched my tent. The sky was beginning to spit, and I quickly gathered wood for the fire. I dragged a downed log up the hill for fuel. It was going to be one of those nights. As the fire grew, I pulled off my boots and propped my feet on the pack for their moment. Beyond the boughs of the fir, rain hit the ground in hard little explosions.

I blanched the Indian turnip in hot water then emptied the water, added the mushrooms and seared in the pan until the turnips were golden brown. With some soy sauce, salt, pepper, Tabasco sauce, and a pack of salmon, I added pasta. As the mixture bubbled, I sliced the mustard root and some ginger into it. I nibbled a corner of the chocolate, took a sip of the Southern Comfort and recalled how good that beer had tasted. The forest darkened before the approaching storm and night. The fire snapped. The smell of my stew wafted in the midst of scents of loam and dirt and rain. I was back in the woods.

My father loved food. He reminisced about great meals the way other people recalled favorite vacations. He spared no expense when it came to food. His rationale was the memory and taste of a good meal would linger long after any material object purchased had been abandoned, broken, or replaced with a newer version. When Keegan was two, my dad served him his first lobster. That started a two year stretch of explaining to a screaming toddler that happy meals didn't come with lobster. By the time I was nine I had eaten dim sum, sushi, thai curry, vindaloo, abalone, squid, brains, and tripe.

I ate my stew by firelight as the wind howled above me. The food was good although I had gone a little heavy on the ginger. My father might have liked it. Merlin would have said it sucked and then taken another serving. I wondered how he was doing. I lifted the whiskey bottle toward the dark sky and took a slug.

"Cheers, Dad."

I didn't know how I felt about his death yet. I had not seen or spoken to him in years. In terms of my daily life, the news changed little. I would get up again the next day and hike. He was a heartless bastard at times, and his favorite hobby had been pointing out my errors and shortcomings. Still, he had his moments, and I had always thought we would share another meal, argue about its preparation or seasonings. One time, just after I was out of basic training, he came to visit, and we went to an all you can eat seafood buffet. Oysters, shrimp and crabs were displayed on broad, mirrored platters with ice. We ate until they were out of oysters and shrimp and asked us to leave.

The rain fell in wide waves, driven by the wind. The boulder and tree kept me dry and the tent still. I scraped the last noodles from the bottom of the pot, put a little water in it, and set it by the fire to boil away the food scent. Another sheet of rain dropped out beyond the boughs. I pulled on my rain jacket and grabbed the food bag and rope. It wasn't far into the deluge before I found a good, horizontal limb and strung the food up into the sky. Raccoons might still get it, clever bastards, but a bear wouldn't.

I dragged the log across the fire to burn it in half and took another sip of the whiskey. During my senior year in high school, we traveled to Las Vegas for a national wrestling tournament. I took second, but the team won, and my father bought us a fifth of Jack Daniels to celebrate. He figured one bottle among twelve boys wouldn't do much. We had the cleverness to get a bum outside a grocery store to buy us several more. Cocky teenage boys with no body fat and lots of alcohol didn't mix well. I came to that conclusion when I ran naked past my mother while she was playing slots and security was chasing me. My father gave me the usual stern lecture for that one, but he almost seemed pleased while he did it.

The fire cracked and snapped. Sometimes an errant raindrop made its way in and hissed with a puff of steam upon landing. He taught me to stir fry when I was about sixteen. Heat the oil in the wok until it is snapping. Drop in the vegetables in a cloud of steam and toss quickly. He was disappointed when I switched my major from English to Business Management. Through tenacity and hard work, he was successful at most things he tried, but he was a vagabond. He had been a hair stylist, police officer, ski instructor and general contractor, and he wasn't happy that I was choosing a career that required wearing a tie. I wondered how he would feel about my current endeavor.

I remembered him carving graceful and effortless turns through fresh powder at Alta and showing me how to tie a double fisherman's knot. We never climbed together. He was already beyond his climbing days when I took it up. I would have liked that. He would have bitched about bolts being a cheating shortcut for driving pitons, but he was grudgingly pleased when I led an unbolted 5.12. He still said the equipment was so good now that anyone could do it. And I went out looking for other achievements that might impress him.

I took a long drink from the bottle. The darkness pressed in around the firelight like a warm sleeping bag. I thought of other happy memories of my dad. There were plenty of unpleasant ones, but it would do no good to dig those up. Given the circumstances of our relationship and my life, a good meal and thinking of him by a fire in the wilderness were the most honor I could offer him. I looked up at the reaching limbs of the fir tree. Bad news does not travel through trees. The boulder loomed solidly behind me, and the reflected fire danced on its face.

• • •

Dawn came to the dripping and saturated forest. I watched the slow lifting of the veil and sipped coffee. An occasional remnant of the storm would pass with a burst of wind that stirred the clinging rain water from the trees. It fell in a flurry of splashes and disturbed the silence for a few moments. It seemed normal; a forest in the morning after a storm. I was attentive to normal. There were no unicorns or talking animals, and the woods were not painted in garish colors. It would have pissed me off if my mind had decided that a unicorn was the way to fuck with me.

Water rolled down the line holding the food bag up in the air. The bag hung like a soggy cocoon. I untied it and let it drop to the ground with a splash. Ziploc bags were a great invention. While other engineers were creating polymers or more explosive missiles, one came up with the idea of a plastic bag with a seal. He was a genius. I emptied out the food bag and dried off the exteriors of the plastic bags, wrung everything out, and packed it all back together dry. I had learned a lot since that first soggy day on the trail.

I broke down the tent. I had set it up and broken it down so many times I could do it blindfolded. I knew because one morning I had done it with a blindfold to see if I could. I buried the ashes from the fire, carefully covering them with soil, and scattered the rocks from the ring. With everything in the pack, the only trace of my presence was the dry rectangle of earth where the tent had been. I considered the metaphor and looked around at the boulder, the big fir tree, and the forest sloping away. I knew I was stalling.

"Rest in peace, Dad." I lifted my pack.

It was a slow slog that morning. The trail was a line of puddles, pools and sucking mud, and I sloshed along through the long green tunnel. Each fern I brushed against shared some of its collected rainwater, and it soon soaked through my gaiters and down into my socks. Wet boots and socks a few months before had created blisters like bubble wrap on my feet. Now, the hardened mass of calluses just scraped amid the moisture.

Around midmorning I came up behind another hiker. His external frame pack was orange, and he wore green pants and a sky blue rain jacket. He hiked slowly, pausing to stare at a tree, moving along, stopping to pull a leaf from a bush, then carrying on.

"Coming up behind," I yelled when I was still some ways back so as not to startle him. Day hikers did not grasp that concept of trail etiquette. He stepped to the side of the trail, stopped and turned. He looked to be in his late twenties with curly brown hair coming out from beneath his multi colored knit hat and the scruffy beard of someone who had been on the trail for a while. He was a little chubby though so maybe he hadn't been out that long.

"Halloo," he said.

"Morning,"

"They call me Jester." I could see why.

"I'm Polar," I said out of habit as I passed. "Have a good hike."

He fell in behind me. Although I picked up my pace, it seemed he could move quickly when he wanted.

"You headin' to Springer?" he asked.

"Maybe."

"You don't know?"

"Nope." I skirted a wide puddle in the trail. He splashed right through it behind me.

"That seems odd, to not know where you're going."

The trail began switchbacking up a steep hillside. I kept up my pace. Although I could hear him gasping behind me, he stayed close.

"Are you going to stop for some water?" he asked between heavy breaths when we crested.

"No."

"You seem to be in a big hurry for someone who doesn't know where he's going," he said from further back. I kept moving. Jester stayed behind.

The sun broke the cloud cover in late morning. The chilly, grey day immediately improved a little. I passed a white blaze on a tree. How many blazes had I passed? I pictured them stretched out, like a meandering path of ants, for hundreds of miles behind me. The terminus loomed ahead. There were only a couple hundred miles in front of me. A gaggle of geese, in a ragged formation, honked above. I slowed my pace.

I paused in a clearing where several oak trees had been felled. I didn't know why someone had felt the need to cut down those trees in that place, but they had created a spot worth investigating. I dropped my pack and scrambled among the soggy logs and stumps. Hen of the Woods was one of the first mushrooms Merlin taught me to identify. Large and looking vaguely like a loofah sponge, they did not have any similar appearing poisonous relatives. It was hard to fuck up and kill yourself with a Hen of the Woods. I found a nice one, about five pounds, growing from an oak stump. It had grown around a branch, and it took a few minutes to carve it free.

Jester's splashing and heavy breathing announced his arrival before I saw him. He came puffing into the clearing as I was cutting the mushroom into pieces to fit in a plastic bag. He smiled when he saw me.

"I thought I lost you," he said. I continued cutting.

"Is that a mushroom?" he asked.

"Yes."

"How do you know it's not poisonous?"

"It might be." I smiled.

"I hear mushroom poisoning is a painful way to die."

"They all are."

"Huh?"

"There are no easy ways to die." I lifted my pack. "Have a good hike."

Of course, he fell in right behind me. We were on a ridgeline, high in the Smoky Mountains, and there were no pending inclines to lose him on. I stopped short, he bumped into me, and then I walked again.

"That's morbid," he said. "You've apparently thought about the subject."

We walked in silence for a while, just the sound of boots in mud and Jester's heavy breaths.

"How would you like to go?" he asked.

"What?"

"If you could choose, how would you die?"

"Soon, and by mushroom poisoning."

"Did you come out here to die?"

I stopped and turned to look at him. Beads of sweat ran down his face, but he still had on the multi-colored knit hat. I started walking again. If I was hallucinating him, I was going to be really pissed off at my mind.

"Are we going to stop for lunch?" he asked. I cringed that it was already "we."

"I'm not."

The trees had thinned. Mist clung thick to the valley below making the ridgeline feel like an island rising from the sea. At a flat slab of rock I heard Jester's footsteps stop.

"I'll catch up with you later," he called as I pressed on. The trail gave a specific challenge to extroverts and social people. Hours and days of silence and only one's own head for company became oppressive. They were the ones who clustered into packs, plodding along in a herd and offering solace and comfort to one another. They seemed not to understand that some of us, the ones who used to read a book during recess, liked being alone.

Without the thud of Jester's boots and his gasps behind me, I walked lightly. The trail wound through massive boulders. I clambered up a few to gaze down at the rising tide of mist. The monochrome grey of the fog surrounding the island peak was offset by the bright sunshine above and had a surreal quality. I was leery of surreal. I reached out to run my hand along a limestone rock as I passed. It felt cool and solid. The sun had passed its zenith, and there were probably a few hours until it retired for the day. I could churn out another fifteen miles or so before darkness set in, and get some distance between Jester and me. He would probably hike through the night to catch up though.

Instead, I ambled, pausing to watch twisted, windswept trees or find out what might be on the other side of a boulder. The fog continued to build up the ridgeline. Perhaps the island was sinking. Trees at high elevation had tenacity. Gravity pulled away their water, and they had to grip tightly to the earth against winds and storms. They didn't have the easy life of a tree in a meadow by a brook. The trees I watched that day were survivors. Did they peer about at their sparse numbers and yearn for lost friends? Or just buckle down for another day's struggle against erosion and desiccation?

The sun dipped behind a distant mountain with a last burst of light that gave a pink and orange tinge to the rising mists. I made my camp on the ridge between two gnarled pines. The spot was too south and without enough elevation to be above timberline, but the wind scoured that place. The tent fluttered in the rising wind. For that night, I would hold the vigil with the trees. I sat on a low limestone ledge and tended to the fire that whipped and snapped in the wind. The wind kept the mists at bay. They lingered down the hill unable to advance. The stars began to roll out in the sky above. The North Star, always first, flickered in the purple dusk. Then, the Big Dipper came into view. I pulled my hat down over my ears and waited for Orion.

Jester arrived first. He was covered in mud.

"I fell," he said while grinning. He was shivering, and the mud gave his multi colored garments a splotched, sickly appearance.

"Get close to the fire." It would not be a quiet vigil.

He smelled like pottery as the fire dried him out. When the shivering had subsided, he went about setting up his tent. It was orange with a green rain fly, and it flapped in the wind while he fumbled connecting the poles. I added wood to the fire and watched. Eventually he figured out to stake the upwind corners first. When it was finally erect, he stood and held his arms up.

"Ta da." Then he bowed.

"Why didn't you camp down off the ridge?" he asked. I looked at the twisted and leaning pine next to me.

"I like this spot." The three stars of Orion's belt appeared low on the horizon as if the hunter were peeking over the distant ridge. I reached out and touched the sea grass rope tied to my pack. Jester began to speak, but I held up my hand to silence him. I realized that I could not walk far enough to escape the hunter's view or even my fellow humans. Jester spoke immediately when I finally looked away from the stars.

"What's the connection between the stars and that rope?"

"Are you hungry?"

I poked at the fire to stir up some coals and stuck the pot in it. When it was hot I tossed in the chunks of Hen of the Woods and a couple packets of soy sauce. The mushrooms steamed and sizzled. I lifted the pot and tossed it to flip the contents. While I cooked, Jester began unpacking the contents of his food bag. He pulled out cans of beans, cans of soup, and a full-sized bottle of salad dressing. I looked at the twenty or so pounds of food he had piled on the limestone.

"What?" he asked.

I dumped the steaming mushrooms right onto the limestone slab. Their aroma was nutty and woodsy. More than most foods, mushrooms conveyed that they came straight from the earth.

"Mushroom?" I offered and picked up a chunk with my fingers and put it in my mouth.

"Are you sure they're safe?"

I put my hands to my throat, opened my eyes wide, made a retching noise and started to twitch. Jester stared at me. Then, I stopped and picked up another piece to eat.

"That wasn't funny."

I shrugged and stirred the fire. Sparks blew into the night sky and briefly mixed with the stars. Orion had risen and stood over us in all his glory. I had looked up at him so many times, but it had been a long time since I had really seen his magnificence. He would hold the vigil with the trees and me. In his ceaseless hunt across the sky, it had been just an instant since Keegan had stared up at him in wonder. Betelgeuse, the star that marked his right shoulder was nearing the end of its life. While still millions of years away, those were just moments on the celestial clock. I wondered if he knew his end was near. Did it give more urgency to his hunt, or did he ease up to reflect?

"Orion," Jester said. He had placed a can of chili in the coals and was trying to figure out how to get it out now that it was hot. He burned his fingers touching it and hopped about with his hand in his mouth. I grasped the can between two sticks and lifted it onto the slab.

"Thank you," he said and sat down with his thumb still in his mouth.

"That's Orion," he said again.

"I know."

He shoveled a spoonful of the chili into his mouth. I prodded the fire again and leaned back to gaze at the sky.

"It doesn't help, you know," he said.

"What?"

"You can't escape whatever you associate with the constellation by staring at it." He had dropped chili down his shirt where it mixed with the dried mud and the bright colors of the fabric. The wind howled through the stunted pines, and the fire was stretched. King Lear and his fool sat in the tempest.

"I don't want to escape it," I said looking down into the whipping flames.

"There's the rub."

The wind continued to gain force. The tents flapped and shuddered in the onslaught, and the fire barely kept its life. The trees stood implacably, Orion looked down, and I held my spot on the ridge. Jester, for his part, seemed untroubled by the gale. He went off a few feet to piss and did it facing the wind. He came back with wet pants but still a smile on his face.

"Aim downwind."

"Yeah." He rummaged in his pack and pulled out a bag of marshmallows.

"Really?"

"What's camping without marshmallows?"

I was envious. I wished I was like him; easily amused. Jester was out there to fall in the mud and roast marshmallows. I accepted the mostly burnt marshmallow he offered me and looked at the tree. Maybe some levity was a nice break from the vigil. I fished in my pack and dug out the remaining chocolate bar. I gave half to Jester, and he broke it in two pieces and squished his marshmallow between them. He stuffed it all in his mouth and grinned while the wind whipped at his face.

· · ·

A black cloud of smoke poured out from under the hood. I turned off the engine and coasted to a stop on the side of the road. The smell of burning oil came into the cab of my truck. I looked at the letter sitting on the passenger seat. The gist of it was that the university had agreed to honor my full ride scholarship in spite of eliminating the wrestling program due to Title IX, all I had to do was remain in good academic standing...and I had failed to do so. Next to the letter was my grade report with the 1.4 GPA. Next to that was the bill for the current semester's tuition. The smoke continued to rise from the engine block and drift across the street.

My gaze followed the drifting smoke to an Army recruiting sign. "$25,000 for college" it announced. I took the registration out of the glove box and pulled off the license plates. I didn't know about vehicle identification numbers. I walked across the street and joined the Army. Later, a psychiatrist would say that was my first manic episode.

I had no idea of the process and thought I would be shipped off right then and there. Instead I took a bunch of tests and caught a bus home. By the time I got there, dinner was on the table, and my little sister announced that an "army guy" had called several times for me.

"I joined the Army," I said. My mom had made curried chicken with peaches. It was one of my favorites. After the initial shock, my mother cried and my dad said he was proud of me.

The recruiter called again that night. I had maxed out all their tests, but I was color blind. As such, the only job available to me was infantry. Apparently, seeing the right colors was not a requirement for killing someone. I said fine and later learned that it was an early lesson in getting screwed.

A week later I reported to Ft. Benning, Georgia. They shaved my head, gave me an automatic weapon, and made me do lots of pushups. Letters from home and friends all said how proud they were. The Army gave me medals and commendations. Sometimes I wondered whatever became of the truck.

· · ·

I crawled out of my tent and into the wind while the stars were still glowing. It had been a long time since I slept through the night. Orion had wheeled across the sky, and just his upside down belt was visible on the western horizon. Jester was snoring in his tent. Some small animals had come to investigate the smells in the night. Jester's chili can was thoroughly cleaned. Just remnants of the marshmallow bag remained pinned under a rock. I zipped up my jacket, pulled my hat down low, and looked at the trees.

They stood resolute and impassive. I had failed in the vigil. The first general order in the military was to stand the post until properly relieved. The trees didn't need me, but I wanted to stand the watch with them. I gauged the width at their trunks and estimated we were about the same age. They had stood there for forty some odd years. Every one of those fifteen thousand or so nights, Orion had looked over the horizon and greeted them. I had failed in my one night sharing the load.

I lighted my stove and made coffee. I could at least stand the post for the cold hours before the dawn. The mists in the valley had dispersed in the night. Far below, a light turned on in a farm house. It was past the harvest and before the sowing. I wondered if that farmer rose so early for any reason other than habit; or if he was unable to sleep like me. He would be making coffee and a hearty breakfast; fuel for a hard day. I would make oatmeal and have an energy bar; fuel to cover distance. He would have something to show for his efforts come nightfall; a plowed field, a repaired fence, or a painted barn. I would pitch a tent twenty or so miles further down the trail.

Some would consider it an accomplishment.

A pine cone skidded across the hard earth, pushed by the wind. I remembered productivity; at least that definition of it. I remembered staying up late on Tuesday nights because that was when the market share reports were distributed. At two a.m. on a Wednesday morning, I would be poring over spreadsheets and exulting in a two tenths growth in yield index. I was still capable of discerning and exploiting the hidden truths in those statistics that others did not see. I just didn't care enough. Given such a report then, I would have stuffed it in a Ziploc bag and been happy for a fire starter. The raccoons that stole my food did not care about my understanding of price elasticity.

The two pine trees stood in silhouette against the sky and stars. They were twisted, gnarled, and leaned heavily to the leeward side. They had lived a hard life on that ridge. Did they ever want to say "fuck it" and just fall over? Maybe that was why there were only two of them. The taller of them was maybe ten feet. I had guessed they were about forty years old from the trunk diameter. Maybe, with the harsh conditions, they were much older. Even at forty, a pine at lower elevation would be towering and straight. I hoped the trees I stood the watch with on that ridge laughed their asses off when that lower elevation tree was cut down to become a telephone pole. Probably not. They just leaned stoically into the wind.

The sun was about ready for its entrance. Orange and purple glowed on the horizon. I often wondered what colors I couldn't see or misinterpreted. Maybe the sunrise was all green and red and fuchsia. I broke down my tent and packed up. The wind continued to thrust across the spine of mountain. The trees continued to stand. Deep down below, a tractor moved across a field. The farmer was about his day. I jotted a note and pinned it under a rock on the limestone ledge.

Jester, enjoy your hike. Aim downwind.

• • •

The trail dropped down the mountainside in a series of switchbacks. Once out of the wind, it was noticeably warmer. The path was thick with pulpy leaves, and I descended with care. It was a slippery slope. That made me laugh, and the sound carried through the still, morning forest. I liked that word "pulpy" and its specific connotation of wet and mushy consistency. Lop was another favorite. Other than a head, there were very few things that could be lopped. I sidestepped down a steep section, prodding ahead with the stick. Plethora was a good word: a polite way to suggest a shitload. I enjoyed the moments when my mind wandered to inconsequential things.

A brook gurgled at the base of the mountain. I pulled out the filter and pumped fresh water into the bladder. In a calm pool created by a fallen tree, water skeeters skated about. I wondered if they got annoyed when the water froze and everyone else could walk on it too. I drank a liter of water and pumped some more to replace it. It had been a while since the desperate, thirsty days of summer and parking lot puddles. Still, I hydrated when the opportunity arose. The water bugs continued to dash about. Wherever they were, they seemed to have a constant and urgent need to be somewhere else on the pool. I lifted my pack, hopped a few rocks across the stream, and hiked on.

The trail immediately began an ascent up another mountain. I considered that most of my favorite words had the letter P in them and wondered if there was a linguistic reason for it. Perhaps the slightly explosive sound of the letter was just more fun to say than others. A flock of grackles banked in above me and settled into a nearly naked tree.

"That's a plethora of grackles," I said. They eyed me with suspicion. I hiked on, digging my feet into the climb.

The twinge of pain came in the second smallest toe on my right foot. I knew what it was. It was an announcement. I hated the fucking disease. I looked up the trail. The crest was not in sight. I switched the stick to my right hand and kept moving. I didn't like the word "pain" even though it had a P. It wasn't fun to say and had no clever connotations. It didn't care. The flare up came on fast, and each step became more painful. Not wanting to attempt pitching a tent on the side of a mountain, it became a race to get to the top before I was incapacitated. It was a slow and arduous race.

I limped upward leaning heavily on the stick. My inflamed foot was squeezed within the boot. There was a jolt of pain with each grinding step. I rounded another switchback and kept hobbling. Sweat dripped into my eyes. I remembered when I ran marathons; hours of effortless motion. The world narrowed to the hard packed dirt in front of me and the shuffling sound as I dragged the traitorous limb. Tears formed and mingled with the sweat. I did not stop. I was afraid I would not be able to start again. I stepped and grimaced, stepped and winced.

"Fuck you," I said.

My leg throbbed, and I could feel my pulse in my foot. I considered taking Percocet but decided against it. I preferred to be stationary and secure while on narcotics. In a wrestling match when I was seventeen, the other guy broke my nose in the first period. They packed it with cotton to stanch the bleeding, and I continued. Each time we clinched he jammed his head against my nose. I felt the cartilage grinding around, and the blood flowed. I put him in a cradle in the last round and held my face over his so the blood dripped into his eyes. I made another step and another grimace. I wished I could remember his name so I could say "fuck you" to him too.

I turned another switchback and could see sky through the trunks of trees up ahead. It was a few hundred yards to the summit. My whole body felt on fire as the inflamed joints generated heat. My sweating hand slipped on the stick, and I stumbled. The surge of pain was so intense that I vomited. The oatmeal didn't look much different coming out than it had going in. At least some crow would have lunch. I continued my slow path toward the summit. I had crashed once in a mountain bike race and slid down a gravel embankment on my thigh at thirty miles an hour. The friction completely removed the skin in some places, and the muscle beneath was exposed. It looked much like a steak at the grocery store. I rode another ten miles to finish that race. I had always been able to endure physical pain. It was the emotional things that made me walk away from a smoking truck or disappear into the woods.

"You got this, Finn," I said out loud. The incline began to level out, and there were spots that would have been adequate to make a camp. I kept walking, just focused on completing one step at a time. The top of the ridge loomed closer and closer. Tears dripped off my chin, and sweat ran off my nose. I could taste its salt on my lips. The last twenty yards took several minutes of stepping, pausing, and gasping, but I stepped over a rise and saw flat trail ahead.

"Fuck you," I said to the disease and dropped my pack.

• • •

A tree rose up above me. It had two large branches that thrust out from the trunk and turned upward. Without leaves, it looked like a pitchfork. I spent much of three days staring at that tree. The first was in a narcotic induced haze. I had spent a lot of time looking up at trees. Even when the painkillers had taken effect, and I felt their warm glow, taking off my boot was excruciating. I hurled it into the forest. Sometime later I had the vague idea I might need it again and crawled through the thick pine needles to retrieve it. I didn't bother to put up the tent or build a fire that first night. I just lay in the dirt with my sleeping bag pulled over me and pondered the effort required to saw off my foot. I don't know what happened to Jester. I was only a few miles ahead of him, but I was thankful he didn't stumble along. Perhaps irrational, but I preferred to be alone with my pain.

It was another dark night of the soul, as they're called. I had had many dark nights. I was reminded of the platitude that God gives us only what we can handle, and I laughed in the darkness at that. I felt like Candide, but he had the advantage of being stupid. If that was the best of all possible worlds, then God was an asshole. A priest had asked me once who I was to judge God. I replied that I was the victim of his crimes. Either God was a cruel puppet master, or he had left us on our own knowing the horrors we would muster from his creation. He was culpable either way. It would have been easier to be an atheist, but I had a firm belief in a higher power; someone at least winding the cosmic clock. The pitchfork hung over me in the dark.

In the morning I slid on my flip flops. My feet were so swollen it looked like the skin might burst. Figuring the worst was over, I took Vicodin instead of Percocet, and I limped out to gather wood. The inflamed feet felt hot even in the cold autumn air. I picked up sticks and fallen limbs and was jealous of the trees that could shed their parts. The recent rains had left puddles, and I filtered water from them and returned to look up at the pitchfork. The rules out there did not change to accommodate my infirmities, and I was okay with that. A clean, defined set of rules was manageable. People made up their own rules and constantly changed them.

The pitchfork stood implacable in the brisk wind. Tattered clouds passed behind it. I boiled rice. The painkillers removed hunger, but eating was essential to staying alive.

...

I could have walked the next day, but it broke cold and rainy. It was a good day to sit by a fire. I burrowed into my pack and found the yellowed, paperback copy of *The Myth of Sisyphus* I had purchased at a library way up north in Pennsylvania. While the rain droned and the fire sizzled, I considered existential angst and pushing a rock.

I recognized the smooth, efficient gait first. When he was a little closer, I saw the bouncing grey ponytail. I wondered if he was a hallucination. Merlin was approaching my camp.

"Asshole," he said when he arrived.

"Dickhead."

We both grinned. He slipped out of his pack, and I rose to give him a hug.

"What are you doing here?" I asked. He had come from the south.

"There's a lot of people looking for you." He sat on a log and picked up a piece of the mushrooms I had roasting.

"Too much soy sauce," he said.

"You came from the south."

"Frog got word of the note you left a ways back. I hitched a ride to get in front of you."

"Why?"

He ate another mushroom and started to unpack. He pulled out a few squash and a small pumpkin. I noticed he had gained a few pounds, probably from sitting around Three Miles' shop doing nothing but discouraging customers, but he was still thin.

"The trail crosses a farm a few miles ahead," he said.

"No beef?"

"Too big to carry." We laughed at that old joke. He picked up the sea grass rope on my pack and assessed its condition. I helped him run the lines for his tarp.

"You've lost some weight," he said.

"You're getting fat."

I pulled out the half bottle of Southern Comfort, and we sat by the fire.

"Your BSW contacted Frog. I've been chasing you for a month."

"As you can see, I'm alive and kicking."

He looked at my feet but didn't comment. I took a slug of the sweet liquor and felt its warmth in my belly. We sat quietly watching the fire and passing the bottle. I remembered the days hiking together with no more than a handful of words exchanged. A crow settled into the pitchfork. It looked at us with black eyes. They say the crow is among the smartest of all animals. He had probably seen a lot from his pitchfork tree.

"I'm not going to ask what you're doing."

"Good."

"But you need to talk to her."

I poked at the fire and ate a slice of roasted mushroom. The crow watched me closely. So, I threw a piece of mushroom to the base of the tree. He swooped down and eyed it suspiciously before taking a peck at it. He gulped it down and looked at me expectantly.

"Now you have to keep feeding it."

I tossed another chunk to the crow. We settled back in to watching the fire.

"How's Three Miles?" I asked.

"Fat and bitchy. He'll be here in probably a couple days," he said and added, "He's coming from the north," when I looked up at him.

"You have me surrounded."

"The bridge you're on...there's no turning back once you cross."

I considered. Perhaps I was fording the Rubicon. Was the entire journey just to create so much distance, mentally and otherwise, that I could not return? While I had often considered not going back, I had never considered not having the option. I suddenly missed ice cubes and comfortable chairs and the warmth at the small of the BSW's back. I wondered how Quinn was doing in school. She struggled with a willful lack of interest in math and science. I felt an anxiety attack coming on, inhaled quickly through my nose and exhaled deeply through my mouth to quell it. I understood at least part of my conflict. I just didn't want to address it.

Merlin began slicing up the squash. I cut the pumpkin into halves and put them in the coals. He rummaged through my food bag and pulled out the ginger and mustard roots.

"Any Indian turnip?" he asked.

"Nope."

"You suck at foraging."

"Asshole."

"Dickhead."

We put all the vegetables together in a pot with some pasta and a packet of tuna. Darkness settled in, and we scooped out the sweet, pulpy meat of the pumpkin. It had a nice smoky flavor. We ate with sticky fingers and watched the stars emerge.

・・・

A pair of hawks drifted in lazy circles on the thermals. Far below, an unsuspecting rabbit would become breakfast. The leftovers would feed a crow or possum. The leftovers after that would feed grubs and maggots. Merlin and I wandered high on the ridgeline. He occasionally stopped to pull up a root and stuff it in his cargo pocket. Three Miles would never catch us if we pressed south so we killed time. I watched the hawks and waited for the streaking dive to earth.

"You've never tried this one," Merlin said, holding up a bulbous green root.

"How do you know?"

"'Cause it would've killed you." He laughed and tossed it aside.

"What's it called?"

"Witch's Lace. You can tell by the delicate leaves."

I looked closely at the killer plant on the ground so I could identify it in the future. The root looked like a tumor attached to the intricate little leaves. There was a screech from above, and I looked up to see just a glimpse of the hawk's hurtling dark form. Something was about to die. The other hawk remained aloft. I wondered if hawks didn't like to share or if there was some professional courtesy about eating another's kill.

We continued to meander through the forest. The dry leaves crunched beneath our boots. I saw the hawk stooped on the ground and ripping the flesh from a rabbit. Death was a constant in the wilderness. Hell, death was the one constant of life. I thought about peoples' terror of death and the extreme measures taken to avoid it. Was it a product of evolution? A compelling urge to remain alive would certainly be beneficial in propagating our species. Did our social revulsion with death develop from a genetic mandate? I had read that, in the early days of Christianity, people were killing themselves to get to heaven faster. The church, concluding that was an inefficient way to build membership, decided suicide should be a sin. In modern society we were so repulsed by someone wanting to kill themselves that we legally allowed ourselves to lock them up in the name of prevention.

I stepped over the rotting corpse of a centipede. A line of ants was efficiently hauling away tiny chunks of centipede viscera. How did I not get the Don't Kill Yourself gene? Even when not actively suicidal, I was indifferent to dying. In the end, you died. It was a rule. Why dread it? Why avoid it? Psychiatrists had long told me that was the depression speaking; that healthy people sought to live long, happy lives. I found it to be simply rational. If the outcome was determined, it seemed more irrational to try avoiding it. I pulled up a Witch's Lace and looked at its root. I should've asked how it killed you. I didn't like the idea of days of heaving, gastrointestinal pain.

Merlin looked at me looking at the plant, and I dropped it.

We walked along the top of a rocky cliff. It was about a hundred foot drop. I paused and stood with my toes extending over the edge. I couldn't remember how to calculate gravitational acceleration, but it would probably be a few second fall. Since I was going to eventually die anyway, it would be cool to learn how a diving hawk feels in the process. An updraft pressed the cliff, and I swayed.

"Want me to just push you?" Merlin asked.

"Think how a hawk feels."

"That he's going to have lunch, not go splat." He turned and walked away.

I lingered for a few moments on the precipice then followed.

The crow was sitting in the pitchfork tree back at camp. I stirred up the fire, and Merlin cooked rice with the assorted vegetables he had farmed from the forest. Everything bubbled and steamed in the pot amid the pungent smell of smoke. The crow waited. I added a packet of soy sauce. I only had a few left. I'd have to find a Chinese restaurant in the next town.

"It isn't fair," Merlin said through a mouthful of rice.

"What isn't?"

"Killing yourself."

I poked at my bowl of food. A slice of some green vegetable stuck to my fork.

"You're a father, and there's a woman who loves you in spite of you."

I watched a small branch in the fire ignite and wither into ash.

"I know."

Merlin lifted the sea grass rope attached to my pack. He didn't say anything, but the point was not lost on me.

• • •

Screams and giggles permeated the back yard. A gaggle of three year olds dashed about as best they could on stubby legs still not quite fully adapted to walking. The new puppy, enjoying the game just as much, leaped after them, hoping to get a taste of the orange soda residue on their faces. Quinn, in overalls and tiara, demanded that her big brother get on his hands and knees for a horsey ride. Keegan, for about the twentieth time, dutifully complied. Duncan, eight at the time, shot the smaller children with his foam dart gun.

I tended the barbecue and watched the melee. There were still a few balloons that had not been stomped for the satisfying explosion. Most of the crepe paper streamers had been pulled down when Shane had the very popular idea to make a mummy out of a small child. The little boy, a multi colored carnival version of a mummy, nailed his part; pursuing his friends with outstretched arms, a stiff legged walk and the occasional spooky moan.

Sarah managed to herd everyone to the picnic table, and I served hotdogs with ketchup. One three year old girl informed me she didn't eat meat. I looked at the hotdog and considered telling her that wasn't a problem. Instead, I removed the dog and left her a red smeared bun. She was happy. Quinn sat at the head of the table and tried to slyly feed her hotdog to her puppy. He had been named Keadis after the lead singer of the Red Hot Chili Peppers. That was Keegan' suggestion. Quinn had wholeheartedly agreed because it was her big brother's idea. She later told me the Red Peppers were her favorite band even though peppers were yucky.

When all the partiers had gone home riding massive sugar rushes, I held Quinn in my arms, and we rocked in the hammock. Keadis lunged and leaped trying to join us.

"Happy birthday, princess."

She reached a small, sticky hand up to my neck. Since she was a baby, her source of comfort, perhaps some sort of reassurance, was to put her hand on my neck when she was held.

"I gotcha neck," she said.

I tickled her, and she squealed and squirmed. I held her close. In a short time, her hand resting on my neck, her eyes closed. She still smelled like a baby. It was early spring. I looked up at the oak tree we swung from. Its millions of buds were preparing for their grand entrance into the world.

• • •

Three Miles came huffing up the trail. It had been a long time since he through hiked. His old external frame pack made a rectangle about him, like a picture frame, as he approached. He owned an outfitting shop full of the latest gear and was out with a thirty year old pack. I smiled. He reached our camp, dropped his pack, and collapsed onto the ground.

"Jesus Christ! That was a tough eight miles." he said after a few moments.

I remembered the early days on the trail and gasping my way up mountains. Now, I didn't even think much about an eight mile round trip into a town to resupply. Merlin probably wandered eight miles every morning before putting his boots on. Our prisms were constantly altered. I wondered how long I would have to be off the trail before eight miles again became an obstacle.

"Frog says you're an asshole and to give you a hug. I'm going to forego the hug."

I reached over and shook his hand.

"Sorry you're out here for this," I said.

"You kidding? Back on the trail versus wintering in the shop with Frog?"

I considered that it was winter up in the north. I didn't know the date, but they certainly had snow by now. Down in the south, there might be a random snow storm, but we'd mostly get sharp nights, morning frost, and chilly days. Cold was another relative term.

"You're old and fat," Merlin said.

"Yeah? You're old and an asshole. In a couple weeks, I won't be fat. You'll still be an asshole."

The weak afternoon sun of late autumn, perhaps early winter, glowed through the naked trees. I helped Three Miles with his tent while Merlin lounged by the fire. It would be one more night beneath the pitchfork tree.

We sat around the fire. The two elder statesmen of the tribe kept a running diatribe of insults. Three Miles carved slices of summer sausage from a log he had packed in. I watched Merlin. He was older than my father. His skin was leathered from years spent in the elements. His grey pony tail was getting streaked with white. While I knew he could hike me into the dirt while carrying twice as much, in that instance he looked old and frail.

Neither of them spoke about why they were out there. Both seemed happy to be out in the dirt and the raw air.

"That thing weighs three pounds," Merlin said about the sausage.

"That's why we have to eat it, dumbass," Three Miles replied.

"That's why you're fat."

Merlin was essentially a permanent resident of the trail. He holed up with Three Miles and Frog or some other member of the tribe for a few months now and then, but his home was out among the trees. I thought about the similarly tragic events we had in common. His solution was to walk in the woods and not go back. He, however, had nothing to go back to. Was disappearing into the forest better, or even different, from killing myself? Wasn't the end result the same for the BSW and my children?

"Why no beard?" Three Miles asked me.

Besides itching like crazy, I had remained resistant to the scruffy, mountain man beard that was part of the distance hiker uniform. I shaved once a week or so. Three Miles still had his even though this was the first time he'd hiked more than fifty miles in years.

"I'm still a noob."

"You probably have birds nesting in yours," Merlin said. Merlin didn't have a beard either.

"Ready food supply," he replied through a mouthful of sausage.

Merlin skewered some sausage along with some roots on a stick he had sharpened and held them into the fire.

The crow had returned to its spot in the pitchfork tree and looked down on us. Killing myself or becoming a permanent resident of the woods being more or less the same outcome, my options were narrowed. Really, I could return to the world or not. If not, what I did wouldn't really matter.

• • •

We hiked, sort of together, for a few days. Merlin wandered off trail in search of mushrooms and vegetables, and he usually emerged ahead of us. Three Miles fell behind early. I would stop at midmorning to wait for him. He would fall behind again. We reconvened at lunch and at the night's camp spot. I tended the pot, and the two old men chimed in with their differing opinions about what I did wrong. On the fourth day, we went off trail, and hiked into a town.

I stared at the phone. The inside of the outfitting shop was like most others. It smelled of wax and hiker stench. The walls were stacked high with fleece and gaiters, titanium spoons and maps, packs and bags. It was an old rotary dial telephone, and it was hard wired into the wall. I picked up the heavy handset and turned the dial. It clicked off the numbers with a resounding thunk. I didn't know what to say. Three Miles and Ratatouille, the owner of that shop, compared mark ups on freeze dried meals. Merlin wandered around commenting on the poor quality of the merchandise. The last digit of her phone number was a zero, and it seemed to take forever for the rotary to cycle back and thunk.

It rang several times, and I was hopeful for voicemail.

"Hello?" She said.

"It's me."

There was a long pause.

"What is wrong with you?"

I said nothing.

"Do you know how worried I've been?"

I still said nothing.

"You're cruel. Do you know that?"

"I don't mean to be."

"I have the police, the FBI, and your fucking tribe out looking for you."

"Merlin found me."

That seemed to enrage her even more.

"I don't care! Why didn't you call me?"

I had no answer that would be satisfying so I remained quiet.

"Are you there?" she asked.

"Yes." Cans of bear spray were arrayed to my left.

"Are you okay?"

"I guess."

"Your daughter has been calling me. I didn't know if it was better to say her father was missing or just didn't want to talk to her." We were both quiet for a while. I could hear her breathing.

"I picked the pumpkin," she said, "It was almost twenty pounds."

"Did you carve it for Halloween?"

We talked for a while. I told her about the hallucinations and the arthritis flare ups and the death of my dad. She said she'd heard about his death from my sister.

"You're lucky I love you," she said.

"I know." I looked at a rack of stuff sacks. They were yellow and orange and red and looked like Tibetan prayer flags.

"I'm still really pissed at you."

"I know."

"Are you ready to come home?"

"I don't know."

"For as brilliant as you can be, you're a God damn idiot."

"I know."

There was a long period of silence on the phone. Merlin, Three Miles, and Ratatouille were conspicuously in the far corner of the small shop carefully studying crampons.

"I love you." She was crying.

"I love you," I said. I hated that I was causing her pain.

"It's been months. You would have found your answers if they were out there."

I thought about that. It was a reasonable point. I didn't have a reasonable response. I still watched Orion rise and fall most nights. I still grasped at a wisp of rope woven from sea grass. I clung to memories, and I looked up at trees. I woke far before the dawn and bitterly watched the spectacle of sunrise. I was still terrified of a world with fluctuating rules; one where people left.

"There is one question still to be answered."

"Just come home," she said.

"I have to go. I'll call soon. I love you so much. I'm....sorry." I put the handset down on the receiver and stared at the old, hardened plastic.

I struggled to catch my breath. The dense interior of the shop loomed on all sides. I went outside, into the thrusting wind, and gulped in the wild air.

Bad news doesn't travel through trees.

· · ·

The grocery store was like all others; a spectacle of food products. There was an entire aisle of chips. I moved quickly with my basket, grabbing packets of pasta, foil envelopes of tuna and salmon, oatmeal, energy bars and a clove of garlic. I did pick up two crisp, shiny Macintosh apples. Merlin and Three Miles meandered in the corridors enjoying the warmth of the store and the array of foods. I had an urge to get some distance between myself and that town; as if that old, black phone might ring at any moment.

I found them discussing varmint stew with a fat old southern lady. I recalled the possum whose head I bashed in and whose flesh I ate. While they debated the best ways to prepare a squirrel, I looked at shelves of microwave popcorn. The packaging was brightly colored, and the brand names were set in bold fonts. I reached out and touched a cellophane wrapped package. Microwave popcorn was the first thing Quinn had ever "cooked". She and I watched the bag swell and listened to the cacophony of popping. The BSW was not allowed to microwave popcorn. She invariably forgot about it until the smoke alarm went off and the house was filled with the odor of burnt butter. I put the popcorn back on the shelf and left.

Outside, I stood next to a woman in a Santa Claus costume. She rang a bell over a simulation iron pot. I loaded my groceries into my pack. People hurried past and dropped change into the pot, and it clanged with the sound of metal on plastic. A man, talking into his cell phone about not being able to find the "fucking doll", ran into me. I apologized; he scowled at me, kept talking into the phone and walked away.

"Fuck you, then," I said. He turned to look back at me, and I took a step forward. He hurried into the store.

I bit into one of my apples. It was crisp and tart. I could not remember the last apple I had eaten. When I was little, my parents would take my sisters and me apple picking in the fall. It was one of those family outings, complete with picnic basket and camp songs in the car. My sisters bitched about bugs and getting dirty. My mother yelled at me when I climbed too far into a tree. We came home with bushels of apples. Some became caramel apples that we ate while the caramel was still oozing. Others were dried on long strips of wax paper and taken on backpacking trips. Most became apple sauce: chunky, spiced with cinnamon and eaten on cold winter days.

The two old hikers finally left the store. We lifted our packs and set off into the deepening gloom. The ringing bell faded behind us. I munched on my apple and set a hard pace. Three Miles' breathing became labored, but he held the pace. We rose, through the switchbacks, toes digging into packed earth, until we crested in starlight and a slice of moon. Sweat steamed off us.

"Eager to leave?" Merlin asked.

I took a last bite from the apple, looked at it and the memories it brought and tossed it into the brush for chipmunk breakfast.

• • •

I was running out of trail. There were many places to meander. I could probably spend a lifetime wandering the Smoky Mountains. The AT though had played a central role in my journey since day one. It had tortured and delighted me for close to fifteen hundred miles. The trail had been the one constant companion. It seemed unfair, almost adulterous, to consider leaving it. Yet, what do you do when you run out of trail before your journey is complete? It seemed an elemental metaphor of my issue. What do you do when you're done living before your life is over?

I studied the guidebook. I had not looked at it since West Virginia. That was a thousand miles and several crises of faith and sanity ago. We had passed into Georgia which meant there was only about seventy miles of trail in front of me. The seemingly infinite white blazes were reduced to a countable number. That was three days of honest hiking. Hell, I could probably do it in two. I could reasonably drag it out to four. Any more than that would be stalling. A hiker, by definition, has to move. Even a meanderer cannot remain static.

My two caretakers were arguing over the best way to tell if a wild leek was ready to harvest. It seemed the purpose of their mission was just to find me, report that I was alive, and then tag along. They may have added the last part themselves. They were enjoying themselves. I didn't mind their company. With their own stories to tell, they accepted that I was fighting demons as just a matter of fact. There was not the normal human urge to judge, or console, or worse, save me.

"About seventy miles," Merlin said when he noticed me looking at the guidebook.

"Yeah."

"A few days," he said as if he had parsed my thought process.

Hannibal, Napoleon and the Romans never solved the problem of logistics. Perhaps I was walking to my own Waterloo.

· · ·

The house smelled of pine and cinnamon. The tree glistened with red and silver lights reflecting off the shiny glass balls that adorned it. The icicle lights outside the windows shimmered and gave the whole room a warm glow. Duncan and Quinn sat, cross legged, by the tree looking at the presents. They were not allowed to touch so they gazed.

Keegan and I lay on the floor. We had two VCR's, a camcorder, a television and a stereo all wired together. It was our Christmas tradition to take all the home video shot during the year, edit it down, add music, and send out our own holiday music videos. It took us hours and hours. There was Keegan in the waves at Myrtle Beach. There were Duncan and Quinn leaping into the pile of leaves I had just raked. The best shots were always the ones where I just left the camera on and nobody knew it....Keegan rocking Quinn to sleep in his arms....Duncan and Shane reading a book together in the hammock....Quinn drinking out of the dog dish.

We argued about where to stop an edit and what music to set things to. He didn't want the shot of him standing with his fly open. We laughed at memories.

· · ·

I was following a turkey. I had come around a bend and found him standing in the trail. He gobbled at me and moved up the trail. Each time I approached, he gobbled and ran away but never left the trail. His red beard bobbed as he went. The old guys were somewhere behind me so the turkey and I hiked together.

"You're not the smartest bird," I said as he again dashed up the trail. There was probably a crow up in a tree thinking he was an idiot. A hawk circling above might be considering that he was an embarrassment to the avian world.

After nearly a mile of our game of tag, the turkey made a sharp right and ran in a perpendicular line away from the trail. This time he did not stop. He just kept going until he disappeared among the skinny pine trees.

I would miss the constant interaction with nature. There was a sense of belonging, of being part of that world. Could I leave it to return to traffic jams, wars, and politics? Was it even possible? I had changed during my time in the trees. I had read about convicts who served long sentences and immediately committed a crime after their release. The sole purpose of the crime was to return to prison and get away from a world with which they were no longer equipped to cope. I couldn't cope in the first place. It was why I was out in the woods.

I hopped up on a boulder to look out at a sea of green pines. It was an illusion of infinity. There was probably a highway or a farm over the next ridge. Still, from that vantage, it seemed my world of trees did not end. I jumped down and continued walking.

There was a rhythm to the forest and the trail. The stars wheeled across the sky. The sun rose and sank. Leaves unfurled in the morning and closed shop in the evening. A sliver of moon swelled, became pregnant, disappeared, and then began again. I moved within that rhythm. The whole hike had been defined by time and marked by sun, moon, and stars. Squirrels and chipmunks chattered in the bright light. The possums and raccoons emerged in the gloom. There was comfort in the rhythm, in its certainty.

I skipped from rock to rock in a boulder field; some remnant of a glacier passing through eons before. I passed a white blaze painted on a rock. I took note of each one now, and I slowed my pace. Had this meander settled me, or centered me, or some other new age crap? Or had it further alienated me from a world I already hated in so many ways? Odysseus's story ended with his return. The official end of a heroic journey is the return. We never hear about life back on the farm. What happened to them after? Frodo said "fuck it" and left again. I imagined Odysseus, his sandal covered in goat shit, staring longingly out to sea.

A flock of sparrows arced above me. They cut through the air in synchronized formation and settled into a tree to squawk as I passed by. I broke off a piece of a granola bar and tossed it down. The sparrows converged on it. I knew how to quiet sparrows. It was probably not a useful skill in society. Ragged clouds were pushed across the sky. I walked slowly, lingering, picking up leaves and twigs and pebbles, examining them then tossing them back.

There was a twitch in my hand, a reminder of the lurking disease. I thought of the twenty pull ups I had to do every night in airborne school to get into the mess hall for dinner. A cardinal bounced along a branch, and I passed beneath him. He was vibrant in the world of greys and browns. He would find his end soon enough. I thought of Penny throwing loaves of torn bread into the air and grackles descending about her. Her pale skin shining in relief against the cloud of black feathers, she would laugh.

I stepped over a rotten log. It was alive with small creatures consuming its decay. I didn't know if there was a heaven or hell. If they existed, I assumed Keegan was in the good place. He didn't live long enough to really fuck up. My dad, I wasn't sure. For myself, I was pretty confident of where God would put me. I didn't care. I'd been pushing metaphorical rocks all my life. It was good preparation for an eternity of doing so. I hoped we at least got an exit interview with God. He had some explaining to do.

The trail crossed a deserted road. I peered at the ribbon of grey asphalt and its faded yellow dashes. The smooth, even surface felt odd beneath my boots. I stood on the centerline and wondered where it went. Who traveled that road? A semi truck lumbered around the bend ahead. I stood my ground until he honked then I stepped into the forest and continued on. That truck driver had a purpose and a destination. The laws of commerce dictated that he was essential. I kicked a pine cone. It was just as essential.

A few yards into the forest, there was a styrofoam cooler next to the trail. It had been a while since I'd come across trail magic. Someone had written "the end is near" on the lid. Inside were PBR's. I sipped the crappy beer that tasted so good and looked up the trail. I could count the remaining miles on my fingers. I felt my heart rate quicken and a tingling in my fingers; indicators of a panic attack coming. After almost fifteen hundred miles of meandering, I was out of trail.

I remembered my first panic attack. I was on a freeway in L.A. when I received the news that Sarah had gone to Florida to see an old boyfriend. We had been separated one month, and she had managed to find a guy she hadn't spoken to in fifteen years, reconnect, and develop such a relationship that she was flying across the country to see him? My vision had blurred into a tunnel, and my hands went numb. I pulled to the side of the road and hyperventilated as traffic raced by.

About a mile up the trail, there was a sluggish stream and a grove of naked cottonwoods. I pitched my tent. I was ahead of the two old guys, and I hoped they'd take a while to catch up. The weak winter sun was high overhead. A pair of tanagers yelled at each other on a branch. Their red feathers were striking against the blue sky. I didn't know what to do at the end of the trail. It had always seemed comfortably distant. I had carried another beer from the cooler, and I opened it.

I remembered sipping Presidentes with Penny on a Dominican beach and when we had Guinness in Central Park while watching remote controlled sailboats in the pond. A snake rustled through the leaves. I wondered why he wasn't sleeping away the winter but figured that far south maybe he didn't need to hide from the cold. On summer days we would sit on the patio watching the water with cold Coronas. I took a drink of the PBR and looked up at the naked branches.

Merlin and Three Miles hiked in around sunset.

"Not as young as I used to be," Three Miles said.

"You're fucking old," Merlin replied.

"You're older than me."

They continued their back and forth while I cooked a pot of rice and then right through dinner. Merlin pulled about ten cans of beer from his pack.

"Did you leave any?" I asked.

"First come, first served."

We drank beers and watched the stars emerge above us. After a couple beers, the old guys turned in, and I sat waiting for Orion alone in the dark. I would miss them. Orion swung into view, and I held up my can of beer.

"Cheers," I said in a whisper. He didn't respond. He never did.

• • •

The last bit of Appalachian Trail, the segment up to the summit of Springer Mountain, is marked with a stone arch. The stones are worn and smooth. I imagine thousands of hands have touched them as they passed through the arch. Merlin and Three Miles had continued toward the summit. Their plan was to turn around and do a through hike all the way to Katahdin. I lingered at the arch.

I had set out on a meander with no intention of accomplishment. Reaching the end of the trail, metaphorical angst aside, meant nothing to me. Several day hikers passed by while I sat. Families with children went by eager for a day of adventure in the great outdoors. I hiked the trail for different reasons than most, and it seemed somehow wrong for me to summit Springer. I watched two black beetles fight. Maybe they were mating. I couldn't tell.

After nearly fifteen hundred miles of chasing splashes of white paint, I wandered into the forest, away from the trail. It was a beautiful day. The sky was a radiant blue, and the sun shined brightly. It was warm enough that I took off my jacket. At the edge of a meadow of still green grass, I dropped my pack. A towering pine stretched above me. I unlaced my boots, pulled off my socks, and propped my feet up. Except for a few flare-ups, they had done their job well. The small breeze felt good on my toes. Birds sang somewhere in the canopy above.

I thumbed through the leather-bound journal looking at the poorly drawn images of mountain crags, stands of fir trees, and shelters I had slept in. The four leaf clover I had found way back in New Jersey fell out. I looked at the notes I had written to Penny, Shane, Duncan and Quinn. I wrote some more, several pages, to each of them, took the sea grass rope from my pack, tied it around the journal, and wrapped it up in the pack's rain cover. It could take some time before it might be found. I picked up the cell phone, considered, then shut it off.

A pair of squirrels dash about the base of the pine and scurry up the trunk. The sun is warm on my face. The grass whispers in the wind. I look up at the trees. I look around at how beautiful the world can be.

My name is Finn, and I'm done walking.

THE END

Other Stark House books you may enjoy...

Clifton Adams Death's Sweet Song /
  Whom Gods Destroy $19.95
Benjamin Appel Brain Guy / Plunder $19.95
Benjamin Appel Sweet Money Girl /
  Life and Death of a Tough Guy $21.95
Malcolm Braly Shake Him Till He Rattles /
  It's Cold Out There $19.95
Gil Brewer Wild to Possess / A Taste for Sin $19.95
Gil Brewer A Devil for O'Shaugnessy /
  The Three-Way Split $14.95
Gil Brewer Nude on Thin Ice /
  Memory of Passion $19.95
W. R. Burnett It's Always Four O'Clock /
  Iron Man $19.95
W. R. Burnett Little Men, Big World /
  Vanity Row $19.95
Catherine Butzen Thief of Midnight $15.95
James Hadley Chase Come Easy—Go Easy /
  In a Vain Shadow $19.95
Andrew Coburn Spouses & Other Crimes $15.95
Jada M. Davis One for Hell $19.95
Jada M. Davis Midnight Road $19.95
Bruce Elliott One is a Lonely Number /
  Elliott Chaze Black Wings Has My Angel $19.95
Don Elliott/Robert Silverberg
  Gang Girl / Sex Bum $19.95
Don Elliott/Robert Silverberg
  Lust Queen / Lust Victim $19.95
Feldman & Gartenberg (ed)
  The Beat Generation & the Angry Young Men $19.95
A. S. Fleischman Look Behind You, Lady /
  The Venetian Blonde $19.95
A. S. Fleischman Danger in Paradise /
  Malay Woman $19.95
A. S. Fleischman The Sun Worshippers /
  Yellowleg $19.95
Ed Gorman The Autumn Dead /
  The Night Remembers $19.95
Arnold Hano So I'm a Heel / Flint /
  The Big Out $23.95
Orrie Hitt The Cheaters / Dial "M" for Man $19.95
Elisabeth Sanxay Holding Lady Killer /
  Miasma $19.95
Elisabeth Sanxay Holding The Death Wish /
  Net of Cobwebs $19.95
Elisabeth Sanxay Holding Strange Crime in Bermuda /
  Too Many Bottles $19.95
Elisabeth Sanxay Holding The Old Battle-Ax /
  Dark Power $19.95
Elisabeth Sanxay Holding The Unfinished Crime /
  The Girl Who Had to Die $19.95
Elisabeth Sanxay Holding Speak of the Devil /
  The Obstinate Murderer $19.95
Russell James Underground / Collected Stories $14.95
Day Keene Framed in Guilt / My Flesh is Sweet $19.95
Day Keene Dead Dolls Don't Talk / Hunt the Killer /
  Too Hot to Hold $23.95

Mercedes Lambert Dogtown / Soultown $14.95
Dan J. Marlowe/Fletcher Flora/Charles Runyon
  Trio of Gold Medals $15.95
Dan J. Marlowe The Name of the Game is Death /
  One Endless Hour $19.95
Stephen Marlowe Violence is My Business /
  Turn Left for Murder $19.95
McCarthy & Gorman (ed) Invasion of the
  Body Snatchers: A Tribute $19.95
Wade Miller The Killer / Devil on Two Sticks $19.95
Wade Miller Kitten With a Whip /
  Kiss Her Goodbye $19.95
Rick Ollerman Turnabout / Shallow Secrets $19.95
Vin Packer Something in the Shadows /
  Intimate Victims $19.95
Vin Packer The Damnation of Adam Blessing /
  Alone at Night $19.95
Vin Packer Whisper His Sin /
  The Evil Friendship $19.95
Richard Powell A Shot in the Dark /
  Shell Game $14.95
Bill Pronzini Snowbound / Games $14.95
Peter Rabe The Box / Journey Into Terror $19.95
Peter Rabe Murder Me for Nickels /
  Benny Muscles In $19.95
Peter Rabe Blood on the Desert /
  A House in Naples $19.95
Peter Rabe My Lovely Executioner /
  Agreement to Kill $19.95
Peter Rabe Anatomy of a Killer /
  A Shroud for Jesso $14.95
Peter Rabe The Silent Wall /
  The Return of Marvin Palaver $19.95
Peter Rabe Kill the Boss Good-By /
  Mission for Vengeance $19.95
Peter Rabe Dig My Grave Deep / The Out is Death /
  It's My Funeral $21.95
Brian Ritt Paperback Confidential:
  Crime Writers $19.95
Sax Rohmer Bat Wing / Fire-Tongue $19.95
Douglas Sanderson Pure Sweet Hell /
  Catch a Fallen Starlet $19.95
Douglas Sanderson The Deadly Dames /
  A Dum-Dum for the President $19.95
Charlie Stella Johnny Porno $15.95
Charlie Stella Rough Riders $15.95
John Trinian North Beach Girl /
  Scandal on the Sand $19.95
Harry Whittington A Night for Screaming /
  Any Woman He Wanted $19.95
Harry Whittington To Find Cora /
  Like Mink Like Murder / Body and Passion $23.95
Harry Whittington Rapture Alley / Winter Girl /
  Strictly for the Boys $23.95
Charles Williams Nothing in Her Way /
  River Girl $19.95

Stark House Press, 1315 H Street, Eureka, CA 95501
707-498-3135   www.StarkHousePress.com

Retail customers: freight-free, payment accepted by check or paypal via website. Wholesale: 40%, freight-free on 10 mixed copies or more, returns accepted. All books available direct from publisher or Baker & Taylor Books.